They're battling a love that won't be extinguished.

Chastity Howell has tried to leave Logan Wright in her past, but her heart won't let her forget the man she once loved. Years ago, she made a senseless mistake that devastated both of their lives. Turning to alcohol for comfort, Chastity started drinking and Logan ended their high-school friendship. Now, she's been sober for years and open to a new relationship. But Logan can't forgive her mistake.

Firefighter Logan Wright is a man of convictions, and he's looking for a good woman to share his life and start a family. Years ago, he'd hoped Chastity Howell might be that woman. But the tragedy she caused, and past hurtful experiences, cautions him that she can never meld with his image of the perfect wife.

Watching Chastity's kindness toward some of Harmony's less fortunate, Logan wonders if maybe he's mistaken. Has she changed? Is this the woman who once fueled his desire? But with so much pain and hurt between them, can they ever get beyond the past to build a new future together?

My Dear Readers

Welcome to the fictional town of Harmony, Alberta. Harmony is roughly modeled after Canmore, Alberta.

The Thurston Hotel itself is the brain-child of Mama Thurston, Brenda Sinclair.

The Thurston Hotel Novel Series was a hoot to participate in. I've never collaborated in this fashion before. Eleven authors, twelve interconnected yet stand-alone books. Creating them was exciting. We fed off each other's enthusiasm and shared characters as well as plot ideas.

With so many different views and writing styles; we bickered, we fought, we laughed, and we plotted. Fires, deaths, love, laughter, we created it all.

We hope that you'll visit the Thurston Hotel and check out of these novels.

Happy reading and may you love Harmony and its residents as much as we do!

Hugs,

Katie

To A Tea

A Thurston Hotel Novel Book Eleven

Katie O'Connor

Snarky Heart Press

Print Edition
ISBN 978-0-9881281-8-7

Copyright © 2016 Canada
By Author Katie O'Connor /*Snarky Heart Press*

Dedication

I have to dedicate this one to the fabulous girls in my writing group CaRWA.
(Calgary Association of the Romance Writers of America)
Without you, this book and this series never would have happened.
Special thanks to Brenda Sinclair for leading the parade.
Super-duper extra special thanks to
Win Day and Shelley Kassian
for talking me in off the ledge when frustration overwhelmed me.

Other Books by Katie

Contemporary Romance
Rekindled Fire

Contemporary Romance Series
Heart's Haven Series (Resplendence Publishing)
Running Home
Saving Grace
Building Trust

Erotica/Erotic Romance
The Gift
Corralling the Cowboy
Tessa's Trio

Chapter One

There wasn't a man Chastity Howell hated more than Logan Wright. But then again, there wasn't a man she loved more either. Life was insane when your heart wanted the one person it could never have.

"Chastity, you really should start dating again."

Tea's chuckle turned into a full belly laugh.

"Riley Hamilton, just because you're love-struck and speeding headlong into matrimonial bliss, doesn't mean that everyone else needs to follow suit. And let's not forget that Brock is head over heels in love with you. You guys are meant to be together. Me? I'm not looking for a man."

Inside The Tea Shop, a converted, bright yellow, two-story Victorian style house, Chastity, known to her friends as Tea, sat at one of her shop's eclectic, mismatched tables with her friend, Riley, relaxing and discussing Riley's wedding plans. Tea loved everything about her décor; she was especially partial to her chairs; particularly the high backed, white, day of the dead chair; her patriotic red and white maple leaf one, and the custom-created Star Trek Captain's chair. The variety of seating and table shapes appealed to her whimsical side.

"What about…"

"Don't even say his name," Tea interrupted. "Let's talk about you. I mean, look at you, you're beautiful; you're an up-and-coming professional. I envy your long curly blonde hair. You're tall and thin while I'm stuck with this mousy brown mop and twenty pounds I can't seem to dump, no matter how far I jog. And I've screwed up my life too badly to recover."

"Hey, everyone is different. You're attractive; your shop is successful. You need to forgive yourself for what happened and find a man who doesn't care about the mistakes you made in the past. Keep telling yourself that we aren't our mistakes; we're who they turn us into. You've changed. You're one of the most loveable and generous people I know. The right man is out there for you."

Tea sighed. What was it about people in love that made them want to ruin life for everyone else? She was happy alone; she didn't need a man to complete her. The nagging voice in her mind that she never quite managed to shut up whispered contrary thoughts. Okay, maybe she didn't need a man, but she wanted one. Not just any man, but a specific one. Why did she have to want the one man that was beyond her reach?

Tea looked up when the old-fashioned bell on the front door of The Tea Shop jangled, alerting her to the arrival of a customer. She resisted the urge to groan when she saw who stood inside the entry. Think of the devil...

Logan. Logan Wright. His name echoed in her head, sounding like Bond, James Bond, but with a dark, discouraging twist that made her heart ache.

He paused inside the doorway looking around. Tea's heartbeat accelerated at the sight of his fire department T-shirt straining over the muscles of his chest and arms. Long and lean and sexily balding with chocolate-coffee eyes, he still made her pulse race, even when the rupture between them made her heart ache with loneliness.

She'd hoped to avoid him today, because in spite of her best efforts, she couldn't stop imagining the feel of his arms around her. Hard to believe it was ten years since she'd felt his teenage embrace. The gangly awkwardness of youth had disappeared and been replaced with the solid strength of a fully grown, well-muscled man. And danged if she didn't want to step into his arms once more, to see if his touch moved her like it used to.

Bah. The last thing she wanted to deal with was a blast from her past in the guise of a sexy firefighter who couldn't get beyond the fact that she'd made one huge mistake. Granted it was life-changing, for her and him and his whole family. She was tired of her heart jumping excitedly every time she saw him. If she couldn't have him, she didn't want to see him. Fat chance she had of avoiding him in a town as small as Harmony.

She dreaded the days Logan made the firehall's coffee run. With the fire station half a block down the alley there was always a firefighter popping in for coffee or sweets. Occasionally, she wondered why they didn't travel the four blocks to Mandy Brighton's bakery, Whimsy. Mandy sold a much larger selection of sweets; her cupcakes of the month were to die for. Yesterday, Tea had virtually inhaled September's Summer's End S'Mores Cupcake. She was tempted to pop over today for another one.

Her own shop sold only cookies, squares and muffins, yet the firefighters found their way into Tea's establishment almost daily. Proximity must make a difference.

Cynthia Sheridan called out a cheerful greeting to Logan from behind the counter.

"Cyn, how are you?" He winked broadly at Tea's teenage employee. Her cheeks went from milk chocolate to ruddy with a blush in seconds. Her brown eyes lit with pleasure at the attention. Her tight curls and ready smile enhanced Cynthia's sweet chocolate beauty.

Tea stifled a grimace at Logan's blatant flirting. He flirted with every woman from two to eighty-two. Well...every woman except her. Too often, she felt like he didn't even know she was alive. His knack for making a person feel important was part of the reason Tea was so smitten with him years ago. Now, it irked her because she missed being the object of his flirtations.

"Hi, Riley," he called with a smile and wave.

Riley fluttered her fingers and smiled.

"Chas." He greeted her by rote in a flat, dismissive tone.

Her heart stuttered.

Butternut. She hated his cold indifferent attitude. Would he ever forgive her for what she'd done?

She glanced at Riley before rising and moving to where he stood. He had a full nine inches over her, yet the height difference felt double that. She was average for a woman and generously curved, but somehow she felt small and delicate beside him, even when he ignored her.

"Logan, I keep telling you...I'm not Chas anymore. I left that part of me behind six years ago when I sobered up. I've told you a billion times to call me Chastity or Tea."

"A billion, no doubt. Come on, Chas, lighten up."

She puffed out a frustrated breath. "Seriously, don't call me that."

"Your name is Chastity Howell. Chas for short. And...you are short." He chuckled.

Tea cast a squinting glare at Riley when she laughed too. It turned her giggles to chortles.

"I'm five foot six. I. Am. Not. Short." She enunciated each word separately to be certain he heard it. "Just because you're a giant doesn't mean I'm short. What are you six-two?"

"Six-three, actually." He squared his shoulders and stood straighter, emphasizing the difference in height. "And you're not just short; you're a little short on patience," he added.

Behind the counter, Cynthia laughed aloud. Tea gave her the stink-eye until she returned to work.

"Come on, Tea, it's funny. What happened to the patented Chas sense of humor? In high school, you were a laugh a minute. Did you break your funny bone, or what?"

"Are you here to annoy me, or did you actually want something? Cynthia will be happy to get you whatever you need." She turned her back on him and returned to her seat.

"As it happens, I called the order in and I'm waiting for it."

His emotionless stare was an icicle to the heart. From icy to flirting and back to icy in a heartbeat. She blinked away a tear at the rift between them, a rift she'd caused. Why didn't he see that she wasn't the same foolish, good-hearted party girl that had been smitten with him years ago?

She'd fallen for him when she moved to Harmony when she was ten, shortly after her twin sister died in a crazy accident near their Calgary home. Something between her and Logan had clicked. Their friendship was instantaneous and she'd been naively certain it would turn into something more.

Later, he'd helped her through the loss of her parents. He'd been her rock, the stabilizing influence in her world, keeping her grounded and focused when things got tough. They'd been fast friends spending every spare minute together. Snowboarding, skiing, hiking or studying; it didn't matter what they did as long as they did it with each other.

That was then, and this was now. Logan had gone from confidant to thorn in her side. The night of her seventeenth birthday, on the night of her biggest screw-up, when she had needed him most, Logan had cut her out of his life. Yeah, Logan Wright could kiss her backside for all she cared.

"Go." She waved him toward the register. "Cynthia's got your order." Turning her back dismissively, she hoped he'd go away and stop churning up longings she couldn't control.

"Later, Riley."

His lack of a goodbye hurt. She glared at him over her shoulder as he paid Cynthia and sauntered out of the shop.

"He's so hot," Cynthia declared as the door shut behind him. "If only he were ten years younger."

"He's a pain in my rear and nothing but trouble."

"Yeah, but he is h-o-t."

"I wish he wasn't." Tea exhaled as Logan disappeared around the corner.

"Good grief," Riley piped up. "How did I miss the fact that you've got it bad for him? I thought you were over and done with him years ago."

"Get real, the man is my worst nightmare. One of these days he's going to walk in here for a safety inspection of this old house; he'll find some trumped-up violation and boom, he'll shut me down, just because we're not together anymore."

"Come on, Tea, you know he's not like that. He's a good guy. Besides, didn't you have an inspection recently?" Riley quirked one eyebrow.

"It was almost a year ago. He has the power to ruin my life, and he has it in for me. One crappy review and I'll be out of business."

Riley frowned. "I'm not sure he's a cold as he seems. Sometimes, I see him watching you. There could be something there. You two need to talk over the past so you can move beyond it."

"Nope, no way. Never. Ever. I'm done with Logan Wright. I just want to run Gran's shop in peace and forget he ever existed."

Forget he ever existed? Like that was possible. He invaded her dreams more often than he invaded the shop she'd inherited from her grandmother.

Chastity chatted with her regulars, cleared dishes and wiped down tables later that afternoon. Furtive motion caught her eye. She pivoted toward it. A grubby red-haired teenage girl in bulky clothing snuck past the counter and headed down the short hallway to the bathroom. It was the third time this week the skinny girl had slipped into the washroom. She never made a purchase, instead she crept in while the staff was busy and was gone before anyone could talk to her. Chastity carried the dish pan into the kitchen and hurried down the hall after the girl.

Tea wasn't concerned that the girl used her bathroom without making a purchase. She'd been caught short more than once and had to use the facilities in another business. However, something about the ragged, unkempt, teen tugged on Chastity's heartstrings. Surely, someone that young wasn't homeless. In Harmony, homeless people were almost non-existent, but this girl had all the markings of a runaway and that was a dangerous way to live in this climate. Every day this week snowstorms had darkened the skies, threatening snow. So far, they'd been lucky and hadn't had any, but if winter hit as hard as it usually did, anyone living outside was in danger and Chastity wanted to help the girl if she could.

She entered the women's bathroom and peeked into each stall. Empty. Where had the girl gone? A frigid breeze blasted over her feet as she stepped back into the hallway. She hurried to the back door. It was slightly ajar. Had the girl slipped out the back?

She strode out onto the back porch and scanned the yard. Nothing. She'd have to mention the girl the next time Roger Nallos came in for coffee. As an RCMP officer, he'd know how to handle this. She'd like to talk to Logan about it, but the rift between them stopped her.

***

Persistent banging jolted her from steaming hot dreams of Logan's well-muscled embrace. Tea bolted upright in her bed. Someone was pounding on the door. She listened for a moment. They weren't knocking on the shop door; it was her apartment door. Her sleep-muddled mind couldn't fathom why someone was on her second story balcony trying to beat her door in. Below the din she heard a man calling her name.

Was that Logan?

What the heck? Why would he be at her door?

"Come on, Chastity, open up. Fire department! I know you're in there. Don't make me break the damn door down."

She leaped out of bed, grabbed her bathrobe and slippers, and hurried to the door and flung it open. Logan stood there decked out in his fire gear. Her heart stuttered and her libido leapt into overdrive. He should be on a sexy firefighter calendar. Why was he beating her door down in the middle of the night?

"Come on, Chas, we have to go. The shop's on fire."

"Chastity," she corrected him.

"Can we argue over it later? You have to leave. Now. The shop's on fire." He enunciated each word separately.

She glanced around. The flashing lights of the firetruck created overlapping glares, distorting her vision. Firefighters scurried back and forth in the grass with axes and hoses. The air was heavy with smoke and her yard glowed with an unholy light. Reality hit her like a baseball bat to the solar plexus. Her knees buckled and she wavered on her feet.

"Holy crap! My shop's burning." Blood surged through her, her heart pounded and panic spiked. What if her whole world went up in flames? She pushed past him.

"Oh God. My house!" Her gaze flew left and right. She wanted to bolt. She wanted to rush back inside and put out the fire. Indecision froze her to the spot.

"Is there anyone else inside? Pets?"

"J-j-just me." She shifted from foot to foot.

Logan grabbed her shoulders and gave her a shake.

"Chastity, get a grip. You need to get out of here." He turned her toward the stairs and gave her a nudge forward to get her moving.

She hurried down with him hot on her heels.

"How bad is it?"

"I'm not sure yet. I had to make sure you were safe before joining the fight. Come over here, out of the way." He led her to an ambulance on the street by her side yard. "The guys will check you over."

"I'm fine." She pushed him aside.

"You can't go near the house; you'll be in the way. Bystanders tend to hinder our work unknowingly. And protocol dictates that you're checked over by the paramedics."

"I'm fine."

"Chas…"

She glared at him.

He placed his hands gently on her shoulders. "Chastity, don't fight me on this. I need to get back to work. Let the paramedics check you over and I'll keep you updated on what's going on inside. Please."

She nodded. He beamed at her agreement and turned back toward her home and business.

It took only minutes for the paramedics to ensure that she hadn't sustained an injury or inhaled any smoke.

She watched helplessly as the crew scurried around dragging hoses and equipment. There were no signs of fire upstairs, and her smoke detectors hadn't gone off. If not for Logan beating her door in, she'd never have known about the fire downstairs.

What if she'd slept right through the fire?

What if she'd inhaled smoke and never woke up?

Holy crap, she could have died! She trembled, her knees knocked together. Her stomach lurched; bile rose in her throat. She was going to be sick. Swallowing hard, she sucked down the anxiety.

How had the fire department heard about the fire? Her alarm system hadn't gone off.

Chapter Two

She hopped out of the ambulance and paced back and forth along the fence line. Smoke billowed from inside, and they'd busted down the back door to gain entrance.

Twenty interminable minutes later, a fireman strode through the gate toward her. Even in full gear and helmet, she could tell it was Logan. She'd recognize that confident stride anywhere.

"How bad is it, Logan?" Her hands knotted together in front of her. She shifted back and forth on her feet while he removed his helmet.

"They had to kick the back door in to get inside. We couldn't risk waiting for you to wake up." He paused as if formulating his thoughts.

"How bad?"

"Not bad, the door will be fine, but you'll need a new lockset and frame."

"Not the door." She glared at him. "Are you being deliberately obtuse? How bad is the damage to the shop?" She barked the words at him. Her patience stretched to the breaking point, threatening to snap at any second.

"Oh, that. Not too serious. Just the small room at the back, the one Willow uses for her psychic readings, caught fire. Thankfully, that door was shut, containing the fire. There'll be smoke damage elsewhere though."

"Well, fudge. I can't afford to be closed."

"You'll have to close for a couple days at least while the arson squad investigates the fire," he sympathized.

"Arson?" Her voice peaked and squeaked to a halt. It was her worst nightmare come to life. Logan was shutting her down in revenge for her past sins.

"I'm not saying it was arson, but all fires are investigated." He dropped his gloves and cupped her arms with his hands. "It's going to be okay, Chas."

"Chastity. Damn it. I said call me Chastity or Tea. I'm not Chas anymore. For Pete's sake, I'm under enough stress right now. I don't need your crap." Uncontained emotion washed over her. Anger at his refusal to stop calling her Chas; fear over the damage to her home; and most of all panic over her future. Fury battled for supremacy. It felt like an emotions hailstorm. She bit back a scream of frustration. How could he stand there so calmly when she was losing her mind?

"When can I go back in?"

"It'll be awhile. Typically, you can enter after you talk to the police and a safety check has been completed."

Calm and professional, his attitude pissed her off. Didn't he know what she stood to lose? Didn't he realize her livelihood was at stake? Through the fog of thoughts, a single word registered, deep in her brain.

"The police?" Her voice rose in alarm.

"Routine questions as part of the investigation."

"I'm being investigated?" Anger crept up her spine culminating in a slow-burning rage that threatened to encompass her. "I didn't do anything."

He shook her gently. "Come on, Chastity, stay with me. Nobody's accusing you of anything. It's going to be okay. Breathe."

Focusing her attention inward, she closed her eyes and recalled Willow's relaxation techniques. Sometimes she got herself worked up over nothing. Okay, this wasn't nothing; but panic wasn't helping. Three deep, meditative breaths later, she opened her eyes.

"Will I be able to stay here tonight?" She asked the question that percolated to the top and pestered her most.

"Unlikely. I'll help you get a few things together once they clear the place. If you don't have anywhere else to go, I guess you could stay at my place."

It wasn't hard to catch the reluctance in his offer.

"With you? Are you out of your mind?" She squinted up at him.

"It's just an offer. You can spend the night wherever you want. I do have a three-bedroom house. I was trying to help out an old friend."

"We stopped being friends years ago. It's too late now, that ship's sailed. It won't matter. I doubt I'll sleep anyway."

Another firefighter strode up and removed his helmet. "Chastity, you can come inside and give things a quick look over. Then Logan can escort you upstairs to grab a few things. The damage isn't bad, but you still can't stay here tonight."

"Thanks, Sam." Logan slapped his best friend and supervisor, Samuel Quinn, on the back. "I'll give her a tour before she talks to the investigation team."

"You do that. I'll help clean up the equipment." Sam nodded his approval.

"Let's go Chas-tity." He corrected himself before she could complain. "I'll grab you some shoes and walk you through."

"Shoes?"

"You're in your slippers." He laughed. "I didn't give you time to get shoes."

"Oh. Butternut," she blurted her replacement for an expletive. "I forgot." She hurried toward the house, dodging firemen on the way.

"Slow down," he called from behind her. "You have to be supervised."

She whirled around and poked him in the chest with her finger. His rock hard, solid muscles jarred everything up to her elbow. She stabbed him again out of spite. Neither jab seemed to faze him. "Supervised?" she squawked.

"Chastity, don't make this harder on either one of us. It's procedure. Technically, we don't have to let you back in at all before the investigation is finished. We're doing you a favor here. I know this isn't easy for you. It never is. I'm trying to help."

Her hands dropped in defeat. "Butternut."

"You know it's cute that you don't swear anymore?" He teased.

"Oh. Gah." There were no words for her annoyance at his glib attitude. She pivoted and stepped up onto the porch. He watched while she changed from slippers to shoes.

"I suppose you have to go first?" she snapped when they stood outside the shop's back door.

"I'll follow. Please don't touch anything."

She took a slow step forward, trepidation washing over her. She closed her eyes and grasped for the strength to deal with this. She hoped there was nothing more than minor damage. The acrid smell of smoke and charred plastic clawed at her nose. The air was thick enough to choke on and she barely resisted the urge to gasp for more oxygen. A lung full of soot would only make it worse.

The screen door was torn off its hinges and lay like a drunken soldier on the back lawn. The inside door had been kicked in and lay discarded in the hallway, covered with dirty boot prints. Splinters and shards of the doorframe littered the floor. Her heart stopped for a second and she sucked in a dismayed breath. Crap. Her pristine floors were pooled with dirty water and bits of grass from the yard. Tears welled in her eyes. Her grandmother, Ethyl

Howell, would be heartbroken to see her former home destroyed like this. For the first time ever, Tea was glad Gran had passed on.

Stepping carefully around the fallen door she edged inside. Aside from the footprints, water, and soot on the walls she couldn't see any immediate damage. Another few steps carried her through the back hallway, past the kitchen and into the main room. Smoke still hung in the air, hurting her eyes and clogging her throat. Dang it. This was bad.

"The major damage is in Willow's space." Logan's voice startled her and she inched forward again.

Willow's room was toward the back of the house, opposite the kitchen. Its door hung crooked and blackened. She closed her eyes and sucked in two deep breaths. Once upon a time, the room had been Tea's grandfather's study. Now, she rented the former den to Willow Silver-Leaf who used the space to sell jewelry and Wiccan supplies and for rune stone or Tarot card readings.

"Okay, Tea, you can do this," she whispered to herself and stepped forward to peek into the room.

The carpet was burnt and melted, the walls black with soot and smudges. The remains of the drapes hung in tatters above a scorched and warped table. The window had exploded outwards. Two formerly maroon chairs were virtually unrecognizable and Willow's favorite recliner was nothing but ash and steel. Thankfully, the fireplace appeared intact under a layer of soot…small blessings.

Tea didn't look forward to telling her dear friend and confidant that she'd lost a fortune in merchandise and furnishings. Tears stung Tea's eyes. She dashed them away, blinking rapidly to keep them at bay. She didn't have time for sorrow or pity. She had a shop to put back together.

Grief settled in her throat like a half-swallowed bite of food. "What happened?"

"See that?" Logan pointed toward a well-scorched table littered with shards of broken crystal. "I think that candle holder exploded. That would have sent sparks and burning wax everywhere. Though we can't be certain until the arson squad does their investigation."

"What? That can't be. I blew them out before I went upstairs."

"Could you have missed one?" His voice was compassionate.

"No. I don't think so. Butternut. What do I do now?" Had she missed one? She was certain she'd extinguished them all. Wasn't she? Water dripped everywhere and a cold breeze wafted in through the shattered window. Shivers wracked her body. Her chill stemmed from confusion and dismay, she was numb to everything else.

"We'll board up the window and the door tonight. You'll have to stay someplace else. Chastity, let's get you some clothes and I'll take you to the hotel."

Blinded by tears, she clutched his hand and let him lead her outside and up the stairs to her suite.

"I'll wait while you pack. Don't take too long."

She grabbed an oversized duffle bag from the closet and randomly stuffed things inside without paying attention to what she was selecting.

"Don't forget underwear and your toothbrush."

She turned and stared at him blankly. "What?"

He stepped out of his boots and dropped his helmet and jacket on the porch. He ambled inside.

"It's okay, Chastity. The damage isn't that bad. You're going to be fine, the shop will be fine. I don't think it will take much effort to repair things. Mr. Zed and a teenage girl rushed into the station. I think I've seen her before, hiding behind buildings. They said they were in the alley and saw the flames. Although I don't know why they were together."

"In the alley, this time of night? Weird."

Shivers skittered down her back. She could have lost so much. Tears rolled unchecked down her cheeks. Her chest contracted and her breathing came in gasps. So much damage, so much waste. Her life was ruined. God, she needed a drink.

The thought stopped her cold.

No! There was no way she was going to let this disaster drive her down that road again. She was not going to fall off the wagon. There would be no drinking.

No way! No how!

Not after what happened the last time.

Chocolate! That was the solution.

She stepped away from Logan. "Almost finished. I need to grab something from the kitchen."

She rummaged around in the cupboards and extracted a battered and dented crème liqueur tin.

"What's in the tin?" His voice was hard and accusatory.

She jumped and turned, unable to halt the guilt that flared at his words.

"Nothing," she replied belligerently.

"Chastity, don't lie to me. I can see the lie on your face."

Irate, she threw the tin at his head. He barely caught it. Staring at her angrily, he popped it open and peered inside.

"Chocolate?"

If she weren't so pissed off, she'd have laughed at his shock.

"Chocolate!" She glared at him, hands on her hips. "What were you expecting?"

"Um..."

"Screw you, Logan Wright. I know what you thought. We've had this argument a thousand times, and you're still wrong. I quit drinking. Yeah, I went on a five-year bender after what I did, after I killed Corrine and your mom. But I've been dry for six years. Do I want a drink? Heck yeah. Am I going to have one? Not in this freaking lifetime. I've struggled too hard to stay on the wagon. So take your sanctimonious attitude and stuff it where the sun doesn't shine." She snatched the tin from his hands, clamped the lid on and pushed past him to jam it into her bag.

"Chastity, I'm sorry. I'll take you to the hotel."

"Screw you, Wright. I'll walk."

He growled low in his throat and huffed out a breath. Good. Let him be annoyed. She was getting sick of his crap.

She'd made one colossally stupid mistake, years ago. After a high school party, and a few too many drinks, she'd loaded her nearly unconscious best friend in the car and headed for home.

Memories swamped her; she closed her eyes, willing away the horrific sounds. Squealing tires, crunching metal, shattering glass. Exploding lights and blinding agony and then...nothing.

She'd woken up in a hospital bed with her disappointed grandmother and an angry cop at her bedside.

She'd missed a stop sign and plowed straight into the driver's door of Mrs. Wright's car, killing Logan's mother in a fraction of a second. Drunk and unconscious, Corrine had flown through the window and snapped her neck on impact with the pavement. She'd died without feeling anything.

That had been the beginning of the end. She'd gone from partier to full-blown alcoholic after one stupid, inexcusable mistake. She'd never forgiven herself, nor had Logan. Slowly, with the help of her sponsor and her friends at AA, she was coming to terms with what she'd done, but it felt like he'd never forgive her. It hurt that he only offered her a ride because it was part of his job.

She understood his pain, his anger, but she'd had enough. "I'll walk," she repeated, hoping to drive her point home.

"It's four in the morning and as cold as hell out there."

"So I'll take a jacket. It's barely over three blocks. I'm pretty sure I can get there undamaged." God, save her from obligatory chivalry. She slipped into her coat and boots and fastened them up. She grabbed her phone charger and her keys and stepped out onto the deck.

He followed her and put his gear back on while she locked up.

"I'd really feel better if you let me drive you over. Chas, it's what firefighters do, we look after people."

"Miss Howell?" A voice called from below them.

She pivoted away from Logan and peered down into the yard. Roger Nallos waved up at her. A cop. Great. Just what she needed. She'd had enough of them to last a lifetime.

"That's me." She banked down dismay and gave a sad wave.

"Can you come down? We have a few initial questions for you."

"Yes, sir. Fudge. Butternut. Dang," she muttered.

Chapter Three

An hour later, Roger dropped Chastity off at The Thurston Hotel. The questions had been straightforward enough, even if they were emotionally draining. Roger had taken it easy on her. There was no way he'd compromise his integrity as an officer of the law, but he'd questioned her slowly and easily, giving her time to think and grieve.

"Say hi to Trey and Matt for me," Tea said as she slid out of the car. Roger and two of his brothers had moved to Harmony a couple years ago. With their dusky skin and slender builds, the Filipino brothers attracted a lot of attention from the local ladies. Gentlemen to a fault, they were well respected in the community.

"I owe you a coffee. You've been kind to me during this disaster," Tea said. "Stop by after I get the shop up and running again and your coffee is on me."

"Just doing my job; but I'll gladly accept. I love your coffee."

"Thanks for the ride." She slid out and closed the cruiser door behind her.

Slinging her bag over her left shoulder, she pushed the door open and trudged inside. Tea didn't pause at the opulence of the blue and gold interior. She was equally oblivious to the rich mahogany front desk and elegant chandeliers.

Mrs. Arbuckle hurried up to Tea. "Chastity, dear, are you all right? I saw the lights and heard the sirens. Someone said your shop caught fire? Is everything okay? What can I do for you?" The petite octogenarian wore fuzzy mule slippers and a silk pajama set, with the sash tied crookedly in her haste to determine what was happening when the sirens started. Chastity smiled weakly at the woman she'd known and adored since moving to town. Mrs. A had the most giving heart, even if she was a touch on the nosy side and had her finger on the pulse of Harmony. Nothing slipped past her, even this late at night. Everyone knew her and she had a phenomenal memory for locals and their families.

"I'm okay, Mrs. A. I'm a bit shaken but I'm good. Shouldn't you be in bed?"

"Oh dear, I was; but the sirens woke me and I couldn't sleep after that. That's the worst thing about getting old, aside from losing my Walter. I don't sleep as I used to. Come inside. Let's get you settled." Her blue eyes radiated compassion.

"I'm going to get a room, relax and try and get some sleep." She walked through the lobby up to the front desk and greeted Alan Backus, the night manager. "Hi, Alan, I need a room for a couple of nights please."

"Oh. I wish I could help you, Tea: but we're booked solid for the next few days. Everything is full for the literary convention this week. I don't have a single room available. Do you have a friend to stay with?"

Tea closed her eyes. Nothing like kicking a dog when it was down. "Thanks, Alan. I'll find someplace to stay." She turned away. Willow was away for a couple days so her place was out. Too many of her other friends were newlyweds or just crazy busy. She wouldn't impose on them. And while Logan had offered, there was no way she'd go anywhere near him. He was too tempting by half and completely off limits. She turned and plodded toward the exit.

"Come with me, Chastity. You can shower and sleep in my room. It's a lovely suite and the couch is marvelous for sleeping. Why, I've fallen asleep on it many times myself." She clutched Tea's hand and led her toward the elevator. "If anyone calls looking for Miss Howell, direct the call to my room please." She threw the suggestion over her shoulder toward the front desk without waiting for a response.

She should resist the old gal's machinations, but Tea didn't have any fight left in her. All she wanted was a hot beverage, some chocolate and a hundred hours of sleep.

"Thanks, Mrs. A I appreciate it." They rode the elevator to the sixth floor and entered the suite. Mrs. Arbuckle lived at The Thurston Hotel. She'd sold all her assets when her husband died and moved into the hotel for the company. She was practically an institution in the hotel and around the town of Harmony.

Tea glanced around, noting the comfortable couch and luxurious furnishings. A small round table and two chairs nestled in an alcove by the window. Through the bedroom doorway, she caught a glimpse of a barely rumpled sleigh bed. The suite was elegant and homey at once with plenty of personal touches, including Betty Jo, Mrs. A's fluffy white dog who was snoring on the foot of the bed.

"Get yourself cleaned up and I'll brew up some tea. Thankfully, I have my own kettle up here. Room service is shut down for the night." She made a shooing motion. "Go on, dear. You're stinking the place up."

Tea chuckled weakly. "I won't be long."

"And bag those smelly clothes up. We can send them down to the laundry tomorrow."

Standing under the hot spray, Tea let the tears come. They poured down her face in rivers only to be swallowed up by the water raining from the shower head. Forcing herself into action, she scrubbed herself clean and washed the stench from her hair. She slid to the floor of the tub, and huddled up crying, her arms wrapped around her knees. Shudders of dismay wracked her body and despite the shower's warmth, she felt chilled straight through.

What did she do now? How long would it be before she could reopen the shop? How long before she even got back in to begin cleaning and repairs? Questions battered her mind like physical blows leaving her bruised and beaten.

Knocking sounded on the door, jarring her from her self-pity.

"Chastity, dear, are you all right? Are you okay in there?"

"Y-yes." She cleared her throat. "I'll be right out. I'm finished." She shut off the water and stepped out of the shower. She dried off briskly and slipped into some yoga pants and an oversized T-shirt. Combing her hair, she squinted into the mirror. She looked brutal. Her bawling had turned her eyes red and swollen. Nothing like adding insult to injury, she couldn't even cry pretty. Crap. Well, she was safe here. There was nobody but Mrs. A to see her.

"Well then. Now you smell like lemons; that's so much better." Mrs. A observed when Tea finally left the bathroom. "You must tell me what product you used; I love the scent of lemons. Come sit. I made you some camomile tea." She waved toward the couch. "Sit down dear, before you fall down. And cover up with that quilt. Myrna Tyrone from the quilt shop gave it to me for Christmas last year. She's a darling, that one. So, generous. Did you know she makes quilts for the hospice and for the police to carry in the squad cars?"

Tea didn't bother to answer. The questions were rhetorical. Mrs. A tended to babble to put a person at ease. Tea snuggled in on the couch, braced against one end, her legs drawn up tight and covered with the quilt. Mrs. Arbuckle handed her the tea.

"I didn't lace it with alcohol, though I thought about it. But then I remembered that you don't drink anymore. I've seen you coming and going to all those AA meetings. I am impressed that you cleaned yourself up like that. Your grandparents would be right proud of you. You've done well. Get some shut-eye. I'll go read in my room and leave you in peace. No sense in me trying to sleep now, it's almost morning."

"Good night Mrs. A Thank you for letting me crash here. I appreciate it."

"You are quite welcome, dear."

Tea doubted she'd be able to sleep at all. Sipping at her tea, she nibbled on some chocolate and revisited the day's events. It had been one heck of a ride. Dang it all, she didn't even want to think about the fire. And stupid Logan Wright? Why had she ever believed he was her Mr. Right? He didn't trust her anymore; granted there'd been a point when she'd screwed up royally. The accident had changed both their lives. Maybe she didn't deserve his faith, but he couldn't seem to get over her chaotic past.

It was beyond frustrating. She'd lost track of how many times she'd tried to apologize, and not because it was part of her twelve-step program. She really did regret her actions. She'd taken two lives because she was stupid and felt invincible. Deep inside she'd never fully forgive herself without Logan's understanding.

She set her cup on the end table and snuggled down under the quilt. She really should get up and brush her teeth, but she couldn't muster up the energy to move. She closed her eyes and willed herself to sleep.

She must have dozed off because sometime later she woke up with wet cheeks. She'd almost swear that she felt a comforting hand on her shoulder, like there was someone there with her. Gosh, she missed her grandmother at times like this when she needed a shoulder to cry on. She sniffed sadly. A light, tobacco-scented breeze fluttered over her, leaving a sense of calm and comfort behind.

Pipe tobacco? No. It couldn't be. This was a no-smoking facility. It had to be the remnants of smoke from the shop fire. "Back to sleep, Tea," she whispered to herself and lay back down.

Great, now she was talking to herself. She was losing her mind. The stress must be getting to her. Because she'd swear she wasn't alone. Maybe it was Mr. Arbuckle's ghost; she almost laughed at the idea. She'd heard rumors that Mrs. A's pipe smoking husband haunted the hotel, but it didn't seem likely and she did not believe in ghosts.

Chapter Four

Logan stood behind Chastity, watching as she surveyed the disaster in The Tea Shop. Against his better judgement, he'd accepted the task of letting her re-enter her business.

Her shoulders shook with tears. He wanted to explain that the damage was minimal, they'd been lucky that the fire was caught early. Most of the destruction was from water and would be a simple fix. He doubted she'd listen. The gulf between them was too vast to bridge easily. He'd burned his bridges with her and didn't know how to go about rebuilding them.

"You know, with a couple of extra pairs of hands, you can have this place cleaned up today and be open tomorrow or the day after. Well, except for the back room."

She pivoted and glared at him.

"This is a disaster. How will I ever clear it up? I'm losing money every second I'm closed." Tears brimmed in her eyes, and his stomach clenched. Her distress troubled him.

"Look on the bright side. The arson investigation is complete. You've been cleared of all wrongdoing. The fire was ruled an accident. You'll only be shut down a couple more days and after a good cleaning, you can open again while reconstruction starts on the Willow's room. All in all, you were pretty lucky that it wasn't worse."

He could almost see the gears turning in her head.

"How did you hear about the fire? My smoke detectors never even went off. And I was dead to the world."

"I thought I told you." He shrugged. "Crazy old Mr. Zed nearly broke the firehall door down trying to get our attention. He was with that girl. They saw it through the side window. He said he heard the window explode from the heat. He should have woken you first, but I guess no harm done." It was lucky that Mr. Zed had passed by at the right moment.

She glared at Logan. "He's not crazy! He's...confused. He's a harmless old man who's had a tough life. Give him a break. I think I've seen that girl around. She's been in the shop a few times. Thank goodness, they were there. The damage could have been worse."

"You should run them off, don't let them hang out around here." The presence of two unidentified homeless people concerned Logan. It wasn't that he believed they were dangerous...he just didn't like the unknown. Mr. Zed had issues; rumor had it that he wasn't right in the head. A shard of guilt stabbed Logan in the conscience; who was he to judge a man he knew only by sight and reputation?

"Why? Why should I run them off? I think they're harmless. Why doesn't anyone see that? Everyone assumes the worst of people they don't know. Mr. Zed's confused. He was a POW, you know. I think he's claustrophobic, but not dangerous. And she's in some sort of trouble and needs some kindness and understanding. Thank goodness, they were around to catch the fire. My gosh, if it had gotten out of control I might have died."

She wavered on her feet and his hand shot out to grab her. "Hold on there. Steady. You can't think about what might have been. Focus on the good," Logan advised.

"I'll have to cook him a nice lunch and give him some extra tea and cookies, or do something special to thank him. Do you think he'd go see a therapist if I paid for it?" She waved off his answer. "Probably not, I'll think of something. And the girl, Logan, we have to find her, so I can help her."

"I'll keep my eyes open for her; but don't worry about them, or the damage, just focus on the good," he repeated his earlier advice, hoping it would penetrate this time.

"The good?" She screeched. "What's good about this?"

He'd stepped in it again. Sometimes talking to Chastity was like walking through a mine-field. You never knew when the next explosion was coming. It made him uncomfortable, even if it was partly his fault for being unable to get over his mother's death.

"The good." He tried to keep his tone calm and non-confrontational. "You're okay. Mr. Zed is okay. The girl is okay. Your apartment is fine. The shop sustained only minimal damage. There's a lot of good here if you search for it. Didn't your grandmother always tell you to look for the good?"

Chastity sighed. "Do you have to be so logical? And quoting Gran is unfair."

He flashed his best rogue grin, the one that always made her laugh. True to form, she chuckled reluctantly. That was better. Years ago, her reward would have been a peck on the cheek, but there was no way he was going there. He didn't want to remember the feel of her skin under his lips. He'd already slipped up and almost kissed her the other day. He was going to have to watch himself. That part of their relationship was over and he wasn't going to open old wounds. His or hers.

"That's my girl," he teased. "Now fetch me a mop and bucket and I'll start scrubbing."

"Why would you do that? Not that I'm turning you down."

He bit back a frown wondering why he was offering to help. They had nothing between them but pain and animosity. After he lost his mom, he'd become a firefighter to help people, and Tea needed help, even if she was the cause of his mother's death.

Tea searched the broom closet for a second mop.

He felt compelled to explain why he was there, even if he didn't fully understand it himself. "Truthfully, I have the day off. I've got nothing better to do. Besides, many hands make light work."

She gave him the disbelieving stink-eye. He held up his hands in surrender.

"No ulterior motive. I promise. Can't I assist an old friend?"

"We're not friends, anymore."

The pain in her voice bounced into a soft spot in his heart and lodged there.

"Then let me help out, as a customer who needs his coffee."

"Fine."

Oh yeah. That was bad. When a woman said 'fine' she meant she was anything but fine. Well, damn the torpedoes. He was going to help whether she wanted it or not. His mother would have expected it. He took the mop and pail from her and headed to the utility sink to fill it.

"Is Cynthia coming in to clean?"

"I can't afford to pay her without money coming in."

"Well then, it's a good thing I'm here." He winked over his shoulder. "You start in the kitchen. I'll start in the main room. Thankfully, the smoke damage is minimal. It's more smoky stench and pooling water than anything else."

When the bucket was full, he filled a smaller basin for scrubbing tables and wiping down walls. He popped open the utility window to let some fresh air in. Behind him he could hear Tea opening more windows. The place reeked.

This wasn't what he'd planned on for today, but Tea needed help and his errands would wait a day or two. He didn't enjoy laundry anyway. He set to work wiping down walls and tables and scrubbing the floor before he returned the tables to their proper positions.

"That triangular table in the front corner is new."

"I found it at an antique show in Chestermere. It fits that spot perfectly. I couldn't resist since they were practically giving it away. I had to refinish it. I counted seven layers of paint on top of the maple."

"You did a good job on it." He paused to wipe his brow. He was working up a real sweat here. Who said that women's work was easy? "Who's doing the repairs?"

"I called Harmony Construction. Mac'll be by tomorrow to start an estimate."

"That's good. They do good work. You'll be pleased with them. How's it going in the kitchen?"

"Like crap. I hate having to throw away all this food, but with the power off for twenty-four hours, I can't take a chance that it's tainted. So everything gets pitched and every single surface gets scrubbed clean and all the dishes go through the dishwasher." She paused. "You know I really appreciate you helping out. It would take forever to clean this up alone."

"Where's Willow? I thought she'd be here helping out."

"Vacation. She's spending a week in Vancouver with her folks. I haven't told her about the fire yet. No sense ruining her holiday. I don't know how I'm going to tell her about all her lost inventory. She had a lot of stuff in her room. Some of her personal items were in a glass-fronted cabinet that protected them from the water; there's just smoke damage and I've read a couple articles on the internet on how to de-smoke books. But one entire shelf of merchandise is gone."

"That's going to hit her hard. I know she'll take it well, though. She's good about keeping calm."

"She had insurance on her contents, because the furnishings were hers. She wanted to create a certain ambiance. I let her have her way because she's a good friend and it didn't interfere with my vision for the shop." She shrugged sadly. "Maybe I should call her?"

"She'd probably appreciate it. If nothing else, she might want to get the insurance stuff started." Strangely, it felt right to help Tea out of this mess. He'd been uncomfortable when Sam told him to let her back in, but that unease was fading.

Tea picked up the cordless phone and dialed. She wandered outside to hold her conversation in private. Logan wished he could be there to support her; this was going to be hard on Tea. Well, if she'd wanted him to hear, she wouldn't have left. He resumed scrubbing.

Five tables later, Logan dropped his rag into his bucket; it was time for clean water. He ambled over to the shop's small kitchen. Peering through the doorway, he almost choked to see Tea bent over, scouring the inside of the industrial refrigerator. He hadn't heard her come back. Her legs were straight and her backside pointed directly towards him.

Damn.

She did have a fine, sexy ass. That ass had been his undoing when she was fourteen and he was a randy sixteen-year-old wanna-be-stud. She was the first girl he ever noticed and she'd been stuck in his head since. Even the issues between them never managed to stop his attraction for her. Whoever said there was a fine line between love and hate was right. He hated her for what she'd done, for who she'd become back then, but a tiny corner of his heart was stuck on her, maybe even a bit enamored with her.

He warned himself not to look; but couldn't tear his eyes away from the delectable sight. She had the sweetest curves. His thoughts drifted back to high school, to that one time they'd made love. It had been hot and sweet with her, better than it had ever been with anyone else. Too bad she'd changed...

"Are you staring at my butt?" she blurted.

"No!"

"You, Logan Wright, are a terrible liar. Get your eyes off my backside." She turned toward him, hands on her hips, her chest heaving in indignation. Her breasts rose and fell in time with her agitated breaths and his pulse quickened in response. Double damn. It was burning up in here.

God, she was lovely. Fit and curvy. She'd outgrown that stringy stage all girls went through. She was stunning with eyes the color of melted chocolate and those golden highlights in her brown hair. Damn!

"Jeepers, Logan. Stop staring. Men are such jerks."

His gaze flew to her face. She was beyond annoyed.

"Are you going to help out here, or ogle me all day?"

"I wasn't staring. I was....thinking. Yeah, I was thinking."

The bell over the front door jangled.

"Saved by the bell," she muttered, her words echoing his thoughts.

"Tea? Where are you?" Cynthia called out. "Hi, Logan."

"Hi, Cyn." He winked at her. "What brings you here?"

"I came to help clean up." She gestured towards her holey jeans and stained T-shirt.

"I can't afford to pay you, Cynthia. I'm sorry." Tea exhaled noisily.

Logan heard the genuine regret in her voice.

"Did I ask you to pay me?" Cynthia laughed. "It's a teacher professional day. There's no school. I'm bored; all my friends are working. So, here I am. Put me to work, boss lady."

"You really don't have to do this," Tea demurred.

"No, I don't. But the sooner this place is cleaned up, the sooner you open and I have my job back. I need the money, there's an adorable pair of red suede shoes in the mall and I have to have them. So I need you to open again." She grinned impishly and laughed.

"Don't turn her down," Logan begged. "This is too much work for the two of us alone."

"Are you sure?" Tea asked Cynthia seriously. "You don't have to."

"I'm sure. I *need* those shoes. Where do I start?"

"The kitchen's too small for the two of us. You could help Logan out there."

Cynthia executed a neat salute and turned to Logan. "Boss me around."

"I've got the walls all washed over here. You start on tables. I'll do floors, and then put tables back. That work for you?"

"I'll get clean water. That's gross." She waved at the bucket he'd intended to change out before getting distracted by Tea's backside.

They worked for hours, cleaning, straightening and restoring the place back to rights. They weren't done by any stretch, but by five o'clock, he'd had his fill.

"Ladies, let's wrap this up. I'm burned out. Let's get cleaned up and I'll take you both to dinner at Pasta Italia."

"Yippee." Cynthia exclaimed. "I love their linguini."

"You don't have to do that." Tea gave him a questioning glance.

"You're right. I don't have to. But I know you. If we don't leave now, you'll keep working all night. So we're taking a break and grabbing some food. I'll meet you guys back here in forty-five minutes. Be ready. I'll call ahead and reserve a table."

"I'll catch you there," Cyn chimed in. "It's easier for me if I have my own ride."

"Sure," Logan agreed after glancing at Tea to ensure she concurred.

Deciding that discretion was the better part of valor, or maybe that retreating was safer, he headed out the front door.

As he climbed into his pickup truck, he wondered what in hell he was doing. Why was he taking her, or them, out? His relationship with Tea was over. Long since over. Her drinking had pushed him away, exactly as his mother's had driven his father away. He didn't need that. Nobody needed to build a life with an undependable alcoholic, especially not the one responsible for his mother's death.

The nagging voice in the back of his head reminded him that she claimed she'd been clean and sober for six years. Could it be true? It didn't seem likely that one could go from full on alcoholic to completely dry without a single slip. His mother sure hadn't maintained any semblance of sobriety.

Chapter Five

Tea flipped through the casual dresses in her closet. It was crazy that no smoke had penetrated her apartment. That was a blessing in an otherwise crappy situation. Everything upstairs could have been ruined. Guess she could count her lucky stars for that.

What to wear? How did she choose? Why did it even matter what she wore? This wasn't a date. This was three people getting together after a hard day's work. Jeans and a sweater would work. That would be the logical choice, but somehow, she felt like celebrating the survival of her personal belongings.

That was it. She'd dress up and celebrate...not because this was a date.

Eventually she settled on a slimming black sheath she'd picked up at Sleek Chic. The local ladieswear shop's owner, Katherine, had fabulous taste in women's clothing and always had something special. It wasn't often that Tea could afford expensive new dresses, but she'd been unable to resist this one when she'd discovered it while helping Riley choose her wedding dress. Gosh it was hard to believe her best friend's nuptials were just months away.

She snipped the tags off the dress and slipped into it. She loved the way it tamed her curves and clung suggestively without being blatant. And the silver beads trimming the rounded, scoop neckline and hem were to die for. They gave it a touch of whimsy and playfulness. It made her feel confident and strong. In addition, she'd need every bit of her strength if she were going to spend an evening with Logan.

Why she wouldn't let him go, she couldn't even fathom. He had no use for her, their friendship was hit-and-miss at best, but her heart still adored him. She'd treasured the boy he'd been, and she loved the man he'd become.

"Stop it." She glared at herself in the mirror. "There's nothing there, and there won't ever be anything between you." She huffed out an exasperated breath. "You're fine on your own." Besides, the only way to keep him safe and alive was to keep her feelings to herself. His job was incredibly dangerous, and with her bad luck at love, confessing that love would only increase his chances of getting hurt. Too many people she loved had died too early. There was no way she'd add Logan to the long list of those she'd loved and lost. She might not have him, but at least he was alive.

Downstairs, she wandered aimlessly, surveying what they'd completed in one long day. Thank heaven for Cynthia and Logan. They'd accomplished so much together. There was still a mountain of work to do, but the appearance and thankfully, the smell, of the shop had improved immensely. She resisted the urge to lift the heavy tarp Logan had nailed over the opening to Willow's room. She would return tomorrow, and they'd get to work after Willow's insurance adjustor had examined it and started her claim.

A light tapping sounded on the door behind her and she turned and let Logan inside.

"Wow. You look fantastic." He smiled easily at her. "That dress is amazing. It clings in *all* the right places." He winked. "Is it new?"

He winked? Why was he winking at her? He wasn't flirting was he? No. There was no way on earth would he flirt with his mortal enemy. She brushed the thought aside. She was going to enjoy this evening.

"It is new. I stumbled on it when helping Riley search for her wedding dress, and what a disaster that was."

"Her mom?"

"Isn't it always Lilith?" They laughed together.

"It that your bridesmaid's dress?"

"No, I bought another one for the wedding, this was too enticing to resist. And Lilith would pitch a full-scale fit if I wore my bridesmaid dress before the wedding... it isn't done you know."

"Speaking of weddings..." He paused, "I'm going to be a groomsman. Brock asked me awhile ago and I wasn't sure how to tell you. Hell, I wasn't sure if I should tell you. But surprising you with it would make it worse."

She winced. Briefly, she wondered why Riley hadn't mentioned it. She was probably waiting for the right time to warn her that she'd be virtually strapped to Logan's side for an entire day. Great, just what she needed-another night spent with him. Dancing, eating, celebrating. Maybe they'd manage to get along and the good memories would carry her into spinsterhood.

"We can make it work," she said at last. "For Brock and Riley, we can get along for one evening. We managed it today, didn't we?"

"We did," he enthused. "Now, about dinner?"

"Let's go, I'm starved. And by the way, you look handsome tonight." A navy blazer topped his pristine white button down shirt. His jeans were stylish, new and well-pressed. He'd shaved and a hint of the citrus and sandalwood of his aftershave tickled her nose. Dang he smelled great. He was the picture of masculinity, the sight of him made her heart pound, and drove away most of her misgivings.

"I see you styled your hair," she teased him. Even with the tension between them, his receding hairline was a long-standing joke. Once blessed with a full head of dark brown hair, when he turned nineteen, Logan's hairline had started receding. Now he was sexily balding on top and kept the rest neatly trimmed and very short. He had a Jason Statham look to him now. All balding and manly and h-o-t, hot! And those chocolate eyes, they made her melt. She concluded that he was perfect...until she noticed his footwear.

"You're not wearing those are you?"

"What? I love these shoes." He winked at her and smiled down at his raggedy sneakers. Battered and torn, they should have been thrown away years ago.

"How long have you had those? They look like the ones you had in high school." She wrinkled her nose in disgust.

He laughed. "They are the ones I had in high school."

"So I got gussied up in my pretty new dress and you're wearing those?" She eyed the shoes suspiciously.

He let go a big belly laugh. "Actually...no. I have other shoes in the car. I thought I'd see if I could get a rise out of you wearing these. And I did," he gloated.

She smacked him on the arm. "You!" She couldn't even find words to express her pique. His attitude was unsettling. It vacillated between tension, joking, distrust, flirting...this relationship had enough disparities to sink the Titanic. She didn't know whether to hold onto hope or run away to protect herself.

"Come on Chas. Relax."

"My name is Tea! Chas is gone." Why couldn't he get that through his thick skull? "Please, call me Tea or Chastity." She enunciated each word carefully to ensure it penetrated. To her surprise, he seemed chagrinned.

"I'm sorry, Chastity. But you were always Chas to me. That's how you introduced yourself the day I met you.

I can't help it. It's hard to change eighteen years of thinking overnight."

Okay, maybe she understood that, a bit. But no one else in town except Riley's mother had trouble calling her Tea or Chastity. It had been six years since she ditched the drunken sot that was Chas and turned her life around. Why did he have such difficulty seeing that?

"Maybe we should skip this whole dinner thing…" She trailed off.

"But Cynthia is joining us and I promised. And we all deserve it after a tough day of slogging through ash. If we don't go I'll feel like an ash-hole."

She groaned at his pathetic word play.

"Your limo waits." He bowed low and gestured toward the door and then hurried to open it for her.

"Thank you." She smiled broadly at him. It seemed that chivalry wasn't dead after all. She locked the door and stepped off the porch.

A shiny, brand new, blue Ford truck stood in front of the shop.

"Nice truck. Is it yours?"

"She sure is. Silly woman. Did you think I stole her?" He chuckled and rubbed one hand lovingly along the fender. Her skin itched with the need to feel that caress.

"Of course not." She laughed as he climbed in to change his shoes. "I was expecting your old car. You know the one with all the rust and dents."

"I'll have you know that car is a classic 1972 Charger. She's my baby. And she's at the body shop getting the dings banged out of her and a new coat of paint. I finished rebuilding the engine this summer. She's a 400 Mag. She'll be the fastest thing in town. I can't wait for her to be back on the road." His voice was tender and loving and more than a little excited.

For a moment, she was envious of the passion he had for his car.

"I call her Jessie."

"You named it?"

He paused with one shoe half on and stared at her in disbelief. "Of course *she* has a name. All cars have names."

"I wouldn't know. I don't have a car and Gran sold hers just after Grampa died. I doubt she would have named it anyway."

"She. Not it. She. Cars are female."

"Sexist much?"

"Nope. Not at all. It's basic science." He gave her a wrinkled nose, skewed-brow look indicating she was insanely stupid. "Everyone knows that. It's a fact."

"It's irrational." She laughed at his mock dismay.

"Then why do they call winter grill covers bras? Huh? I ask you why?" He hopped out of the truck and locked it defiantly, showing that he'd made his point and won the argument.

"You are aware that you're being totally irrational? Right?" She gave him a quizzical look. She missed their mock arguments. The playful banter had been a staple of their friendship. Even when they disagreed it hadn't been serious. Their core beliefs were the same, only the details differed, but never too widely.

"Let's walk. It's cool but not freezing and it isn't far." Offering his elbow like a gentleman, he led Tea down the street and around the corner to the restaurant.

Logan had reserved a table at Pasta Italia— it helped that he knew the owner, and they were ushered straight to their table by the host. Logan held the chair and she slipped into her seat inhaling deeply. Basil, cheese, garlic, pasta; the aromas made her want to lick the air. The scent in here was to die for.

"I love this place. Just breathing adds ten pounds to my hips and I don't even care. It smells divine and the décor is fabulous." A hand gesture encompassed the entire room.

Marble tile flooring, candles in wax-covered Chianti bottles sat on every table, rich blue walls rose above oak wainscoting. Pristine white tablecloths draped twenty widely scattered tables. A chain restaurant would have put at least another ten tables in the same area. Pasta Italia radiated romance and intimacy. Tea remembered from her previous visits that the food was glorious and the portions huge. She always went home with leftovers. She resisted the urge to rub her hands together with glee. Oh yeah, she loved this place. And to be here with Logan? Sublime. Although she'd never admit it, even to herself, it was a dream come true.

They chatted uncomfortably while waiting for Cynthia to join them.

Inside her small beaded handbag, her cell phone jangled. Who could that be? She pulled it out and answered.

"Well, so much for dinner." She slid the phone back into her purse. "That was Cyn. She's going out with some friends. She's giving dinner with us a miss."

"That doesn't mean we have to skip dinner. Does it?" He appeared perplexed.

"Look, Logan. I know you planned this as repayment for Cynthia because I couldn't pay her to help clean. Repairs are going to cost enough and I don't have anything back from my insurance adjustor yet. I might be on the hook for the whole repair and then for the lost income while I'm closed. My budget isn't that huge. I can't afford…never mind. My problems aren't yours. But without Cynthia, there's no reason to stay and eat." She hoped she sounded reasonable and logical, rather than self-pitying. She could use the evening out, she still liked spending time with Logan, in spite of everything but she didn't want him to feel obligated.

He gave her a questioning glance. "What about you? Don't you want a nice dinner?"

"That's not what I'm getting at." If he would drop the subject, it would save her the trouble of sorting through her jumbled feelings. If she couldn't understand what was going on in her head, how could she expect him to?

"Why don't you and I stay and eat. I mean, we're dressed up anyway. No sense wasting the outfits."

She studied his expression. He appeared to want to spend time with her, but that didn't jibe with his usual attitude. The danged man blew hot and cold and it was driving her nuts.

"Come on, Chas-er-Tea. Let's have something to eat. I'm starving and I hate cooking. You don't want me to go to bed hungry, do you?"

"Well, at least you got my name right." Somehow, that pleased her more than it should. It occurred to her that if she did have dinner alone with him, it would give her a memory of him to hold close when she was sitting in her apartment years from now as an old spinster. One meal. What could it hurt?

"Okay. Since I'm already dressed, and you're here. Let's do this."

"Wow, your enthusiasm is overwhelming." He winked to take the sting off his sarcasm.

She laughed.

"Sorry, that was a bit ungracious. Mr. Wright, I would love to have dinner with you." *Mr. Wright? Yikes! That sounded wrong. This was not good.* "And I meant Mr. Wright, not Mr. Right. Just to clarify."

"Sure," He stretched the word out into two syllables. "That clears it *right* up."

They both groaned at his bad pun.

She glanced around the room nodding politely when she met the eye of someone she knew. She nodded at Mandy from Whimsy and her beau, Kevin MacNeal. Nestled under the window, Bailey Thurston, of the Thurston Hotel Thurstons, was in a serious discussion with Dan O'Leary. The restaurant was packed.

Tea smiled at Logan when he settled across from her in a secluded corner. "Thank you for this. I don't think I could have mustered up the energy to cook tonight. I might have gone to bed hungry because I'm out of peanut butter for toast." She laughed at her laziness.

"Purely selfish motives on my part. I don't have to cook and I get to spend the evening with a beautiful woman."

Color rose in her cheeks. Pleasure battled annoyance. What was with him? Some days he flirted, others he ignored her entirely. It was disconcerting. She closed her eyes and searched for calm. She was going to enjoy this night if she had to bite clean through her tongue to do so. The waiter arrived to take their beverage order.

"I'll have iced tea, please," Chastity requested.

"I'll have the same."

"You do know that I don't mind if you have a drink, right?" She didn't want him avoiding alcohol on her behalf. It had taken almost two years, but she'd adapted to others drinking around her. Although, on occasion, she wished she could partake, in spite of knowing better.

"That's okay; I'm good with iced tea."

The waiter looked back and forth between them in confusion.

"You having a drink won't push me off the wagon," she pointed out. "I'm okay around alcohol now. There was a time when I couldn't have a meal without a beer or wine, but not anymore. Please, feel free to have a cocktail."

He studied her face carefully, like he was searching for something. At length, he nodded and turned to the waiter. "I'll have an iced tea, please." He smiled at her.

She returned his grin with a raised eyebrow.

His hands rose in a stop-gesture. "I have the midnight shift tonight. I don't drink before work. Your being here didn't impact that decision at all. And yes, I do believe you can be around alcohol without drinking."

He spoke the words, but didn't quite meet her eyes. Would her stupid mistake ever stop haunting her? Would she ever live up to the standards he expected? Even a fool could see that he was trying to trust her, but to Tea, it was clear that he didn't quite manage.

Well, she'd prove him wrong. One day he would realize that she was a changed person. She had no intention of ever drinking again. She wasn't naïve enough to think that she'd never have a lapse, but she was certain that her friends and her sponsor, Connie, would help her over that hurdle if it ever occurred.

"Look," She met his gaze. "I know you don't trust I've changed, but I have. Can you please try to give me the benefit of the doubt?"

His hand gripped his water glass until his fingers turned white. She wondered if he was going to snap the stem off. Something must really be stuck in his craw. Finally, he puffed out an exasperated breath.

"Chastity, you know mom was an alcoholic too. She never got over it, in spite of trying repeatedly. AA was no help. Hell, incarceration didn't help. She hit the bottle the day she was released. It's hard for me to believe that people recover from alcoholism. It just kills them in the end."

She reached out and stroked his knuckles until his hand relaxed onto the table. She eased her fingers under his palm and gripped his hand between hers. "Do you want to talk about it?"

"No." The word was harsh and sounded more like an expletive than a refusal.

"Okay. You don't have to. But can I say something?"

"You just did." His poor attempt at a joke fell flat.

"Look, Logan. Nobody ever stops being an alcoholic. There is no cure. That's why we're called recovering alcoholics. It will always be a struggle to stay clean and sober. Some manage better than others. I've been blessed not to have fallen off the wagon, though I have come close. It must have been so hard for you to watch your mom slide deeper into it. It must have hurt you badly. I know what I did is almost unforgivable. I can't ever take it back. I can't undo it. Nothing I do or say will ever bring your mom back. It haunts me every single day. All I can offer is my sincere apology."

He stared down at the table, not acknowledging her admission of guilt.

"My AA group meets every day, except Sunday at the Thurston Hotel. The meetings are private for alcoholics and addicts, except on Saturday. We open those to the public and to people like you who are friends or family of someone with an addiction. Those days we focus on dealing with addictive people in our lives and how to help them deal with the issues and aftermath of their loved one's addiction. You should consider coming by some time. You don't have to take part, you can just listen."

"I don't think so."

"It's up to you. Think about it. Or, I could get you some books to help with the pain."

"I'm not in pain." He denied hotly.

"You are, even if you won't admit it. But more than that, you're angry. I've known you since we were kids. I can read you like a book most of the time. I won't push it, but learning more could help you deal with the aftermath. I made mistakes, your mom made mistakes. We can't undo that, but we can try and get beyond it."

"She's dead. Alcohol killed her." His voice was dead, like he didn't care.

Tea understood that pretending not to care was his way of coping with his loss. But for her, the words were a sword to the gut. He meant that Tea had killed his mom in the end. He didn't say it outright, but the accusation was there.

She squeezed his hands. "I'm sorry for my mistakes, and for your loss, for our loss."

He pulled his hands free of hers, grabbed his glass and downed the contents in several big gulps. "Thanks."

"So, I'm thinking about getting a cat." She changed the subject abruptly. "Remember when I had Mittens? I miss having her sleep on my bed. So I think I might get another one, you know, for company."

He blinked at her in surprise. "Slow down, you'll break your neck changing topics like that." His laugh was genuine.

She shrugged. "I thought it best to move on."

"Can you have a cat? You live over your shop."

"I've checked out the regulations. As long as she doesn't enter the shop, it's fine. The shop is considered an eating establishment and separate from my suite. So, it's all good. I think I'll call her Hot Dog."

"You can't name a cat Dog." He challenged.

"I can and I will."

"Can I take your order now?" their waiter asked, sidling up to the table gracefully.

"Oh. Yeah. I forgot to look at the menu." Tea laughed. "I'll have the spicy calamari appetizer. And for my main course I'll have bow tie pasta Alfredo with roasted chicken and a small Caesar salad, please."

Logan ordered the steak and pasta feast with a large green salad and the Italian Wedding Soup with bruschetta for an appetizer. "We could share appetizers, if that's okay with you?"

"Oh yes. Please. I love bruschetta. I had trouble choosing between the appetizers." She laughed at her own greed. "I won't have to eat for a week after this. Thanks again for bringing me."

He waved off her thanks. "And you can't call a cat Hot Dog."

"I can, and I will. And...when I get a dog I'm going to name it Diogee."

"Dee oh gee? What kind of name is that? What about Spot, or Killer or Rambo."

"D.O.G. If you say the letters in the word dog all close together it sounds like Diogee. So that's what I'll call him." She grinned triumphantly and he laughed.

"You have the most twisted sense of humor that I ever saw. I always loved that about you."

"Why thank you, kind sir." It was at that second that she saw him relax. Finally, he'd let go of his tension. He hadn't forgiven her, but maybe his heart had softened a bit. Now they'd be able to enjoy their meal. The stiffness seeped out of her body as she leaned back in her chair.

It took only moments for the appetizers to arrive. The calamari sizzled in its pan and the scent of the hot peppers tickled her nose. The bruschetta was brimming with fresh tomatoes, basil and onions. They looked divine and smelled even better.

They chatted about what their high school classmates were up to now while they ate. When Logan reached for the last curl of calamari, she stabbed it with her fork.

"Hey, that's mine," she declared.

"I got it first." He snatched it up with his fingers and popped it into his mouth. "You snooze you lose."

Feigning indignation she sputtered, "I'll have you know that I'm famished. I might starve to death without that delicious, spicy morsel."

"Ha. We've eaten enough to feed four people and our meals haven't even arrived yet. I'm saving your hips some extra abuse."

"My hips?" She glared even though she knew he was teasing. She was curvy, there was no sense denying it. Years ago, she used to bemoan those curves but he'd made it abundantly clear that he loved them. She'd grown comfortable with herself and didn't worry about it anymore. "You love these curves and you know it." She gestured at herself.

He laughed. "It's a good thing I'm a fireman or I'd never be able to handle the heat those curves generate." His pupils dilated as he took in her figure.

Her breath sucked in in response. From friendly joking to burning heat in seconds. His gaze fairly sizzled. *Oh my!* Her mind struggled for a light response. Thankfully, the waiter returned to clear their plates and bring them their salad and soup.

After dinner, walking home side-by-side, their arms brushing together occasionally, it felt like the old days, before the tension between them exploded their friendship. "I'll walk you up," he said as they reached her yard.

"You don't need to do that. I'm a big girl."

"True enough, but I want to. I always walk my dates to their doors."

She stumbled on the sidewalk.

"I'm not sure what surprises me most; that this was a date or that you date at all. You don't date. Ever."

"I date, just not in Harmony. I go to the city. Privacy and all that. I'm an authority figure here; I don't need to parade my dating failures around town."

"Dating failures? Now that needs an explanation." She walked through the gate on the side of the building toward the back stairs, with him following close on her heels.

"My dating life hasn't been the greatest. I've tried those dating sites without much luck."

"I know about that, I can't believe how many of them don't resemble their pictures at all. Last summer I met a guy who had to be ten years older and twenty pounds heavier than his picture. When I called him on it, he said he'd had a rough week so he looked tired."

"It's not so much about the appearance, as the lies. I can't tolerate a liar. Or someone without a sense of humor."

"You mean like you...no sense of humor?" She chuckled to herself.

"I'll have you know I have a great sense of humor." He sounded indignant.

"Indeed?" She turned to squint at him with one eyebrow raised.

"Oh. You caught me there." He chuckled. "But seriously, there aren't that many eligible women in Harmony. Bachelors outnumber spinsters by far."

"Spinsters? That's harsh." She grimaced. "I'm hardly a spinster."

"You don't date much either."

"I'm surprised you noticed. It's because I'm not sure what I want in a man, I just know I haven't found it yet," she prevaricated. She did know what she wanted; strong, handsome, intelligent, a good sense of humor, caring, and compassionate. In short, she was looking for Logan but she couldn't take a risk on him, or any other man for that matter. Between getting beyond what she'd done and her bad luck in love, the odds of building anything with Logan were infinitesimal.

"I don't know what I want either, but I haven't found it," he confessed. "It sure wasn't any of the desperate women who showed up at the station after the release of last year's Fire Fighters of Hope calendar. You know...the one that raised money for the hospice?"

"Oh, I know...I have those images burned into my mind." She fanned her face.

"A bad fire pun? That's so beneath you."

"What can I say? Firemen are too hot to handle." They climbed the stairs to her door, enjoying the companionship of shared laughter. The tension between them wasn't gone; it hovered in the background, just close enough to make everything awkward.

"Well, this is me. Thank you for dinner."

"You're welcome. But I do have some dating advice for you." His hand was warm where it cupped her shoulder.

"Seriously?"

"Don't eat garlic on a date, it can be a turn-off when your date tries to kiss you goodnight." His eyes danced with laughter.

"Ah, but tonight my date ate garlic too...in his pasta and his bruschetta. So I'm safe."

"That is true." He studied her for a long, heated moment. The chill of the night air dissipated under the heat of his gaze. He leaned in.

His lips brushed across her forehead, his touch as light as angel wings. He stopped there, his lips on her hair.

She wondered what he was thinking. She fought the urge to lean into him, to encourage him. The bag of leftovers in her hand shifted, almost falling to the deck.

She leaned back and took a small step away.

"Good night, Logan. Thanks for helping me clean up and for dinner. Sweet dreams."

She pivoted away and unlocked the door. She was inside with the door closed in a fraction of a moment. She leaned against it and drew in an unsteady breath. Damn. One tiny brush of his lips and she was a goner. Butternut! Dang and blast! She'd have to double the distance she kept between them.

He knocked lightly on the door and she leapt away from it.

"Good night, Tea. Thanks for the lovely evening. And lock the door."

She flipped the deadbolt knowing he wouldn't leave until she did. There was no sound for several long moments, before she heard his footsteps descending the stairs, the snitch of the gate latch and finally the sound of his truck roaring to life and driving away.

Why did she feel like she'd dodged a bullet?

Chapter Six

A thumping sound from the shop awakened Tea. She rolled over and focused her eyes on her alarm clock. Five forty-five? In the morning? What the heck?

Stumbling into slippers and a robe, she grabbed her cell phone and snuck down the private stairwell connecting the shop to her suite. At the base of the stairs she eased back the deadbolt and inched the door open. The smell of freshly brewed coffee hit her like a wave of energy.

Who was making coffee at this time in the morning?

She crept quietly around the corner to the kitchen.

Willow? Logan?

"What in the world are you doing here at this ungodly hour?" She glared at them.

Ever cheerful, Willow laughed; her smile lit up her face and made her blue eyes dance. Her silver hair shimmered in the bright lights of the shop. While Logan was losing his hair prematurely, Willow had turned fully grey at twenty-three. After several failed attempts to dye it, she'd given up and embraced her natural color. Strangely, the color didn't age her; it gave her a wise, peaceful look. Willow pushed her dark-framed glasses up and hugged Tea.

"Good morning, sweetie." As a full-time employee, Willow had her own shop keys and had let herself in.

Tea grunted a response. She was as far from a morning person as it was possible to get. She barely functioned before a massive infusion of caffeine.

Logan poured a cup of coffee and handed it to Tea. She mumbled her thanks and grasped the mug between her chilly hands, absorbing its warmth and inhaling its life-giving aroma.

"I changed my mind, shortened my trip and flew back to Calgary last night," Willow chimed. "I was fretting about the damage. So I came to check it out. I ran into Logan getting off work and here we are. My insurance guy is coming at seven-thirty."

"And you're here now? Are you insane?" Tea studied Willow for overt signs that she might have lost her mind.

"I couldn't sleep, okay? So I came over to see how much damage there is and to see if anything could be salvaged."

"Should you touch anything before your adjustor gets here?" Tea voiced her concern.

"No, she should not." Logan pinned Willow with a glare that indicated this wasn't the first time he'd had to warn her.

Tea laughed at them both. "My adjustor's been through. Nevertheless, he said you shouldn't enter the room until yours sees the mess. I'm sure Logan can get you a copy of the incident report from the station." It was as much question as statement and she glanced at him for verification.

"Why are you here already?" Tea asked Logan. "Aren't you on midnights?"

"Midnights is an expression. I work eleven to seven. I was on a coffee run when I ran into Willow. The guys know where I am if they need me. Quinn's working on the fire report. The investigation ruled it an accident, but he's not finished all the paperwork. I'll bring over copies before I start my shift tonight."

"Can I peek if I don't go in?" Willow begged.

Tea and Logan shared a glance.

"You have to promise not to touch anything," Tea warned her friend. "There's a lot of minor damage. But I'm not moving until I finish this. Thanks for brewing it by the way. Where did you get the coffee? I haven't even ordered replacement supplies yet."

"I warned her that we had to throw out all the consumables." Logan grinned. "And then I took her to the convenience store."

"I suppose you'll want a bagel too?" Willow waved a paper bag towards Tea.

"Absolutely. Cinnamon raisin?" she asked hopefully.

"How can you even think about food after everything you ate last night?" Logan teased. "I'm still stuffed and I worked all night."

Willow's gaze pivoted between them. She raised one well-groomed eyebrow questioningly. "You guys had dinner together?"

"Not exactly." Tea denied the question.

"Yes, we did." Logan contradicted her.

"Which is it?"

Tea could almost hear the myriad of questions running rampant in Willow's mind.

"You're the fortune teller. You tell us." Tea laughed and tried to quell the telling blush rising in her cheeks.

Willow smiled broadly and tapped her finger on her lips thoughtfully. "Well...I'm going to say yes, you did share dinner. And you both enjoyed it immensely. And, you're going to do it again."

Tea shook her head. "I don't think so."

Logan gave Tea a scrunched eyebrow look.

"Trouble in paradise I see."

"Oh give it a rest already. And hand me a bagel."
She bossed Willow around in the playfully rude way that
only close friends could get away with.

Willow held out the bag obediently.

"Is that new?" Tea asked catching sight of an
intricate silver band on her friend's thumb.

"How can you tell?" Logan asked. "She's
wearing... five?"

"Actually, I have ten on my fingers and two that
never leave my toes. I'm kind of a jewelry addict."

"That's insane," Logan blurted. "And dangerous."

"I take them off if I'm working with tools." Willow
laughed. She held her hand up for Tea's inspection. "Isn't
it great?"

Willow studied the silver ring. A wide band of
linked rounded, three point Celtic Trinity knots circled her
thumb. The knots alternated one point up and one point
down. The top of the ring was a focal point green stone.

"What stone is that? I don't recognize it." Tea
stroked the oval stone.

"Green amber. It's fairly rare. It's a healing stone
and provides psychic protection. It can balance the
emotions and clear the mind. That's why I chose it for
today. My mind is in chaos."

"It's beautiful. Where did you get it?"

"Dad made it. He's been doing some silver-
smithing. I found the stone at a gem shop in Abbotsford.
Dad put it into one of his designs while I was at home."

"It's stunning, can you get me one?" Teas asked.
"My mind could use some clearing."

"You don't really believe that bull shit, do you?"
Logan blurted.

"And what if I do?" Tea's hands fisted on her hips.

"It's...it's...insane."

"Just because you don't believe it doesn't mean it's crazy. There are a lot of ancient stories and legends about the healing power of stones," Willow injected calmly.

Tea stifled a laugh. That was the ultimate Willow. Calm in the face of the storm. She had her beliefs and nobody could dissuade her from them. She was Wiccan through and through and believed in a lot of things that Tea didn't understand.

"It's a beautiful ring. Can your dad make me one?" Tea repeated her question and ignored Logan's expression of disbelief.

"I brought several back to sell; with earrings and pendants to match."

"Ooo, I'll take a whole set." Her smile wobbled and fell. "Crap. I can't. I'm going to be short on money until I figure out what's going on with insurance."

"I'll let you choose from what I brought back once I get my room back together again. I'll hold them for you," Willow offered.

"I can't ask you to do that." Deep inside, Tea did want Willow to save her a set, but she would never ask that of her friend.

"No problem. I don't mind a bit. And, I've got some calming candles at home that you can burn to help you relax and unwind."

"Seriously?" Logan blurted.

"It's known as aroma therapy and it's about knowing the medicinal properties of herbs. It has been scientifically proven that certain scents trigger predictable responses. I've cast candles with different color and scent combinations for different purposes. I sell quite a few of them. Including blue wax scented with lavender for relaxation. Green with patchouli and cinnamon oils for prosperity. The combinations are endless."

"So you're going to waste money on stupid candles?" He shook his head. "Insane. She's tapping into your gullibility to get your money."

"Logan!" Tea glared at him.

"Actually, I'm giving them to her; as a gift from one friend to another. It's what human beings do. You Neanderthals might have a different way of doing things." Willow scolded him in a rare fit of temper. "Oh. Now you've gotten me annoyed. Nobody annoys me." She sounded bewildered.

"I think you should go, Logan." Tea gestured toward the door. "If you're going to insult my beliefs and my friends you don't belong here."

"You really believe all that stuff?" His tone softened, like he was trying to understand.

"I don't know if I believe all of it. But Willow's never been wrong about the effects of the candles she gives me. Besides, I wouldn't rent her space if I thought she was dishonest. Seriously, Logan, lighten up."

"I don't get it." He shrugged helplessly. "I just don't get it."

"It doesn't affect you, why should it bother you?" Willow's logic had returned.

"I suppose..." His tone landed somewhere between agreement and confusion.

"Let it go, Logan." Tea advised. "Go home, get some sleep. You've been up all night."

"You're probably right. I'm overtired. Except for a catnap at work, I've been up for more than twenty-four hours." His brown eyes were apologetic. "I'm sorry, Willow. I don't believe in that stuff, but I shouldn't bash your beliefs. It was rude and inconsiderate." He turned and gave Tea a quick hug. "Good night. Good morning. Or something. I'll stop by later and see if you need any help before I go to work."

"Good night, Logan. Sleep well," Tea said.

They watched him walk away.

"Wow. He's totally balls-to-the-walls gone on you." Willow laughed.

"You, my friend, are crazy. He can barely tolerate the sight of me most days." She wished he were crazy over her; and that their friendship was back to where it once was. Then again, maybe things were best left alone and unchanged.

"Oh sweetie. You are so wrong. When you came in the room, he looked dumbfounded. He stared at you the entire time he was here and not because your robe is open and that flimsy nightgown was drawing his eyes."

Tea snapped her robe closed and tightened the sash. She glanced at the windows to reassure herself that she'd closed the blinds yesterday. She kept them shut at night, opening them was a visual signal that she was open for business.

"He's a perv. All men are pervs."

"Generally, I'd agree with that. A man won't ever avoid that view. But this was different." She twisted her lips in concentration. "He looked like he wanted to eat you up. Not porn-like, but love-like."

"Porn like? That's a new one." She popped a couple bagels into the toaster and rummaged in the bag for the container of cream cheese she knew Willow would have brought.

"You know...that creepy old guy leer. It wasn't like that. It was like he was smitten. That's the word. Smitten. Like Orpheus was obsessed with Eurydice. Tragic and hopeful all at once. Like so many mythological couples."

"Well it's irrelevant. I'm not interested in Logan. Or in any other man for that matter." She grabbed plates for their bagels and Willow handed her a knife.

"We've been over this before you know." Willow placed a comforting hand on Tea's arm. "You've had a run of bad luck. That's all it is, nothing more, nothing less."

"Bad luck?" Tears welled in Tea's eyes. "My sister dies in a freak playground accident. My parents die in a crash. My grandfather died of unexpected congestive heart failure and I killed Logan's mom and my best friend. All between when I was ten and seventeen. Six people I loved gone in seven years. That's not a run of bad luck. It's...I don't know what it is, but it sucks." She sniffed and wiped her eyes on her sleeve.

"Statistically speaking, it's not that out of line. Your grandmother died of natural causes and she's the only one in the eleven years since Corrie was killed. It balances out. I admit that many people you loved died in a short time span, but since then...almost nobody has died. The average is good. Seven in eighteen years isn't bad. Don't take that wrong. I have nothing but the deepest sympathy for you, but it's time to move on and start living again." Willow hugged her tightly and kissed her cheek.

"I can't. I can't get beyond it. I know it's not logical, but thinking of losing another person I love makes me crazy inside."

"What about me? What about Riley? What about all your other friends? I know you. I know you love all of us. You just have to trust in the good in the universe. You have to believe that things will turn out okay and they will."

"I'm trying, really I am. But I've loved Logan since the day I met him when I was ten. I can't let him in. Not that he wants in. I can't risk it. He'll never forgive me anyway."

"Remember what your grandmother told us right before she died? She said, 'Remember the good times but never forget the bad ones. Life is a balance. There is no happy without sad. There is no good without bad.' You've had your bad. Tea, trust me, your good is coming."

"I'll try, Willow. I'll try. But it's not easy."

"I can find you some positive thinking mental exercises," Willow offered. "Although except for this one thing, you're one of the most up-beat people I know. Your optimistic energy is what drew me to you in the first place."

Chapter Seven

With a lot of effort and a few rush delivery orders, Tea managed to get the shop open in only eight days. The work had been extraordinary, but the rush of pleasure when the first customer walked in the door was uplifting. Even Willow's room was up and ready to go, though she was a little low on stock. Mac from Harmony Construction's team had worked double-time to get things put back together.

"Morning, Tea," Dr. Sheridan called out as he entered the shop.

"Hey, Doc. How are you? I've missed seeing you." She smiled.

"I'm better now that you're open again. I've missed my lattes."

She started his drink. "Double shot latte with chocolate sprinkles and a half-squirt of vanilla coming right up."

"Please don't make it too hot this morning, I'm dying for my fix." He laughed for a second and then went serious. "Sorry about that."

"About what?" she asked in confusion.

"For the drug-addict reference. I know you've had problems; I didn't mean to bring up a sore subject." He grimaced.

"No worries." She waved off his distress. "I've learned not to take offence at casual comments, though there was a time that it might have reduced me to tears. The AA meetings help."

"Speaking of which-" a familiar voice came from behind the doctor, "where have you been? We've missed you. I was starting to worry."

Tea hurried around the counter to embrace her AA sponsor, Connie Branch. She loved strawberry-blonde-haired Connie like a mother. She'd been Tea's lifeline since she started climbing out of the pit she'd dug herself.

"Connie, I meant to call you. I've been swamped with repairs and restocking. I'll be at this morning's meeting. I'm good. I managed to stay on the wagon." She returned to fix the doctor's drink.

"Good to hear," Connie and Dr. Sheridan replied in unison.

"I admit it was tough some days. I must have gained ten pounds from all the chocolate I scarfed down." She laughed. "It's a good thing for yoga and my other addiction, jogging. It clears my head and works off the chocolate."

The doctor paid for his drink and two oatmeal raisin cookies, his morning breakfast. He held the door open for Logan who slid inside.

Tea took a full twenty seconds to admire how Logan's T-shirt stretched across his chest and around the muscles of his arm. Dang. He was hot. Her heart gave a little pit-a-pat of joy.

"Hey, Connie. Tea." He leaned over the counter and tugged on a lock of Tea's hair. "I've only got a minute; I'm on my way to work. Want to go for a short hike this afternoon? I get off at four."

"Why?" Tea asked, unsure of his motives.

"Because that's when I get off work."

She could tell his confusion was feigned.

"Because, I'm trying to give you the benefit of the doubt here. I'm trying to find my way past my anger and rebuild our friendship. I talked to Dad last night and he said Mom would want me to move on."

She mulled over his words. Was he serious? Did he really want to rebuild what they'd lost? Did she want to?

"Sure." The word escaped her mouth before she knew her answer.

"Meet you here at four-fifteen then." He smiled and jogged out the door.

"Wow," Connie exclaimed. "That is one hot guy. If I wasn't old enough to be his mother..." She trailed off suggestively.

Tea chuckled and dropped a teabag into a paper cup. "He is at that. But I'm not sure I want to go back to what we had as kids. I'm not the girl I was back then."

"And he's not the boy he was then either. His mother's death hit him too hard. When his father moved to Texas to live with his brother, Logan was all alone in that big house. He still is, except for the dog."

"He's got a dog?"

"It's a white fluffy thing. Not a pup, but not full grown either. He's training it for search and rescue. With Tessa's dog, that'll be three. And the team needs every one of them; especially this time of year when the weather gets unpredictable."

"True. It's been a quiet summer for the team. We've only had a few calls. Fall and early winter mean more work. The team needs to get there quicker to beat the elements. More dogs will help. I wonder why he didn't tell me about it."

"He's a man," Connie laughed. "My husband doesn't tell me anything without prompting. Neither do my three rotten-no-good sons."

"You love the lot of them in spite of their flaws," Tea reminded her.

"And I love you like a daughter. I really was getting worried about you. If I hadn't seen Willow in the bank the other day, I'd have been banging on your door with an intervention team."

Her voice was lilting and teasing, but Tea recognized the truth behind them. She'd been on more than one intervention herself. You did what you had to do to support your friends; and most of her AA associates were friends; some, like former country music superstar, Jade Carter, were family. Jade had lost everything to her addictions and was clawing her way out of the pit she'd dug.

Tea finished prepping Connie's camomile tea and passed it over. "This one's on me. A pathetic thank you for all you've done for me."

"Helping you has helped me stay sober. It's a win-win situation. Thank you. However, you really should stop giving away your product...you'll hurt business in the end. So here." She passed Tea her payment.

Chastity smiled warmly. "I owe you way more than a drink. But I appreciate the support, in all its forms."
***

Tea slipped into her hiking shoes and her wind suit. She hated the way the slippery fabric rustled when she hiked, but the air was chilly and nothing made a hike more miserable than being cold. She said goodbye to Willow and stepped onto the porch where Logan waited.

"I was thinking of heading out Cougar Road into the hills and picking a trail up there. That okay with you?"

"Sure thing. I haven't been hiking all summer."

They climbed into the truck for the short drive to the trails. The radio played softly under their conversation.

"I love this song. It reminds me of your mom." Tea turned up the radio. She sang along.

Logan's arm shot out and switched the radio off.

"I hate that song."

"It was your mom's favorite."

"That's why I can't stand hearing it," he snapped as he pulled into the first set of hiking trails. The truck lurched to a stop and he jumped out before she could respond.

She was out of the truck and at his side in seconds. "Logan, are you okay?" She placed a hand on his forearm. He jerked his arm away and used the remote to lock his doors before storming up the trail. He raced away as if demons were chasing him. Understanding his need for solitary thinking, she followed at a more leisurely pace after grabbing her small pack from the truck box. He disappeared around the first bend in minutes.

"Well," she huffed aloud. "That went swimmingly."

Eventually, she caught up with him.

She crested the third hill and came face to face with the back of his head. He was sitting on a boulder staring ahead. Pausing, she studied him. His shoulders were tense and his back ramrod straight. Memories of his mother and the accident must be gnawing at him. Tea scrambled up a rock adjacent to his perch and settled in to study the valley. She didn't speak; he'd open up when he was ready.

She pulled her water from her pack, took a drink and handed it to him. He drank deeply, consuming nearly half the bottle. Good thing she'd packed several, he'd left his in the cab of the pickup.

"Sorry," he said gruffly, without looking at her.

"Apology accepted."

"Just like that? Without even asking for a reason?"

She heard, rather than saw him turn toward her.

"Just like that," she agreed and swung her knees to face him.

He wasn't crying, but tears had left moist tracks down his cheeks. Not once in all the years she'd known him, had she ever seen him cry, not even at his mother's funeral. He wasn't the type of man to show his feelings; he dealt with them internally and moved on when he had them sorted out.

"I'm sorry for mentioning your mother," she offered. "I didn't mean to open an old wound."

"Forget about it," he ordered softly. "It wasn't deliberate."

She'd poked the sore spot between them unintentionally. Regret squeezed her chest.

She edged forward on her rock, leaned in and kissed his cheek before sliding off the front of the rock and wandering down the trail. She kicked idly at a rock in the path and kicked it again when she reached the place it landed.

A small creek ran through the valley, and she settled on a sandy space to toss pebbles into the water. The sun shone warmly and the earlier wind had stilled to nothing. She slipped out of her jacket and stretched out to stare at the sky. The sound of his footsteps approached and her eyes drifted shut.

She wasn't going to push him; she'd wait this out.

Rustling told her he'd shed his jacket and dropped it on the ground. She peeked out through slits in her eyes and watched him settle on his coat, his thigh brushing hers. A deep frown turned his mouth down, his eyebrows scrunched together. Her heart clutched; he looked sad and broken. His face was a tight mask echoing his emotional turmoil. His hands scraped across his face and up over his head knocking his hat to the ground. He sat there, elbows on his knees, his face buried in his hands.

She moved without thinking. Sitting up, she slipped her hands between his arms, edging them aside, exposing his face. Fresh tears glimmered in his eyes. She realized that this went deep; it was about more than an old country song and memories of his mother. His distress battered her heart. Instinct kicked in and she leaned in and pressed her lips to his. She meant to comfort him, distract him and relieve his burden. Torn between empathy for his pain and passion, she deepened the kiss. He didn't respond.

"Oh, Logan," she whispered against his mouth. Her voice cracked on the words.

His hands fisted in her hair and pulled her toward him. His lips crushed hers taking everything she had to give. He tasted divine. Coffee, mint and man. Her blood pounded in her ears.

Pouring every ounce of sympathy and love she had into her embrace, she wrapped her arms around him; her hands stroked his back and shoulders.

Heat exploded through her. Even her fantasies hadn't measured up to the reality of his lips. It had been years since their one and only passionate encounter. They'd been little more than children then, but this? Sweet heaven, she hadn't expected the swamping onslaught of emotions that surged through her. His urgent response touched her mind, her body and the secret spot in her soul that she protected from everyone.

What was she doing?

She pushed against him.

"Logan, wait. We can't do this. I can't do this." She pushed out of his embrace. "Can we talk about it instead?"

"There's nothing to talk about," he denied, rising to his feet.

"I think talking about the accident, and what you feel might help."

"Chas, I don't want to talk. I'm done. We're going home." He pivoted on his heel and headed back to the truck.

Her heart ached for his pain, for his inability to get beyond the past; but darn it, her body ached too. She loved him, she wanted him, but not like this. Not in anger with a thousand unhealed wounds between them.

Chapter Eight

After three nearly sleepless nights Tea crawled, bleary eyed, out of bed. These crazy dreams of making love to Logan had to quit. Now.

He hadn't forgiven her, but his anger had eased a bit and they were less uncomfortable around each other. Unfortunately, that wasn't enough for her. As much as she loved him, she couldn't take the next step in their relationship without his forgiveness.

Making love with him would be the easy way out. She didn't have the strength to survive the aftermath of casual sex with him, and she refused to compromise, even if it disappointed Logan.

It wasn't his style to push her; he was much more subtle than that. He kissed her at every opportunity and never missed the chance to touch her. Those simple touches had the power to leave her wanting more. She needed him and it took every ounce of her strength to resist.

Casual physical relationships weren't her thing. There was a time, when alcohol clouded her judgement, that she was careless about sex and had earned the brutal teasing she'd taken about being totally opposite her name. Chastity had flown out the window. She'd remained careful about safety, but not so much about whom she slept with.

Those days were long gone and good riddance to them.

She showered, dressed and stumbled downstairs for a much-needed infusion of caffeine. Today's cookies wouldn't bake themselves. She could get the first batch into the oven while she main-lined coffee. The drug metaphor didn't escape her; it made her chuckle. There was no doubt that she was completely and totally addicted to her morning brew.

Stepping into the shop, she noticed the front porch motion sensor light was on.

Seriously? Who was up at this ungodly hour? And why were they here? It was too early even for the newspaper delivery guy.

The man standing outside the door didn't even have to turn around to face her. It was Logan. From her dreams to reality, there was no escaping him. She shuffled to the door and flipped the lock off. She headed for the coffee pot without opening the door or greeting him.

"Not awake yet," he chimed happily, locking the door behind him.

"Gah."

"No sunny smile or kiss this morning?"

"Seriously? Why are you so chipper this morning?" She fumbled with the filter and started the coffee. "It's stupid o'clock in the morning and you're all smiles and chuckles. Morning people make me sick."

He laughed at the familiar refrain.

"Boy, I remember those high school mornings. I'd pick you up and hand you a coffee when you got in the truck. You never said a word until you'd downed half a gallon of that go-juice." He chuckled. "Cheer up, Tea. It's a lovely morning."

"According to you," she growled.

He stepped into the kitchen and slid his arms around her waist, resting his chin against the back of her head. "Good morning, beautiful."

His lips were soft and warm against the skin of her neck when he nuzzled her ear. She shrugged him off.

"Too early?"

"Look, don't get me wrong." She turned to face him and pushed him away. "We're not going there."

"I can't kiss you?" Annoyance colored his words.

"It's too soon, Logan," she said sadly.

"Chastity, we're both adults."

She poured them each a coffee, trying to formulate the proper response. Her eyes drifted shut as she enjoyed that perfect, first sip of the morning. She could almost feel life returning to her body as her mind awoke.

"Don't overthink this," she advised cautiously. "We used to have…something, then we were…estranged," she put the most positive spin she could muster on their break-up. "Now, we're almost friends, but we do not have an actual relationship." Sipping her beverage, she offered the second cup to him.

He snatched it out of her hand, sloshing hot liquid over his fingers. "Damn it. That hurt."

Did he mean the words, or the hot liquid?

He wiped his hand on his pants and looked at the floor. "We could have one."

"We could. There's too much anger between us. You haven't forgiven me and I can't make you; but if you don't find a way to let it go, we can't ever build anything. There's no trust. Without trust, there's nothing. Nothing at all. And I won't sleep with you, as much as I want to, until we have an actual relationship." Oh great, why had she admitted to wanting him? Good grief, she must be losing her marbles.

Butternut!

Now she was flustered, aroused, over-tired and felt stupid.

"But you do want to?" he asked hopefully.

She glanced up at him; his eyes glimmered with hope. She had to turn away before that optimism swayed her into making an unfortunate decision. He'd always been able to talk her into anything.

She rummaged in the industrial fridge for the rolls of refrigerator cookies she'd prepared the night before. "Turn the oven to 350, please." Placing a cutting board on the counter she started slicing the dough as she formulated her next words.

"It's not that easy," she hedged after a long pause. "I do want to. You're important to me. But I'm worried that if we rush into this we'll ruin any chance we had of making it work. I don't want to start anything without the possibility that it might go someplace."

"So if it isn't permanent you aren't interested? That's a far cry for the carefree girl you were," he snapped.

Someone who didn't know him well might think he was angry, but Tea recognized the hurt and confusion in his voice.

"I'm not the girl I used to be," she said patiently. "And I'm not the untroubled teenager I was before I ruined our lives, and I'm not the drunken slut I was after that. I've changed, Logan. I know that's hard for you to understand. Hell, sometimes I'm amazed at how different I am now." She slapped come cookie rounds haphazardly onto a baking sheet.

"Logan, I like you. I do. But unless you can find forgiveness, we can't have a relationship. A friendship is strain enough, anything more is…impossible."

"I…"

She held up her hand in a stop motion. "Don't. Don't speak, please. Just go home, take some time and think about it. Clear your head. And when you're ready, come back and we'll talk."

He took his cup to the sink and rinsed it. His motions were stiff and tense, and she read the pain in his bunched muscles.

"Logan, wait." She wiped her hands on a towel and walked to him; his back was rigid, his shoulders tense. She turned him to face her. His arms crossed over his chest.

"Part of me is still the teenage Chastity who loved you. You're special to me. I'd like to date you, to spend time with you and see where it goes. I've changed. You've changed. I think the best thing for this...relationship... if that's the right word, is to start over. Have a couple dates and learn if we're still compatible. We haven't shared more than a few words since the accident."

She pressed a finger to his lips, forestalling his argument.

"I know my drinking had devastating consequences and I drove you away. I can't alter that. We can't change the past. However, we can change how we act in the future. So think about it. Decide if you want to take a chance on me. I understand that you don't believe that I've stopped drinking, but I have. Only time will prove that to you. What happened was an accident; it was totally my fault but not deliberate.

"Your mom was like a mother to me; I know how horrific it was, and I feel the aftermath every single day of my life. I'm trying to forgive myself, and hope you can try as well. So go, think about it. But know that I won't sleep with you right away if we start dating again. I don't sleep with the other men I date either, no matter what you think."

"Chas...Tea. I want to believe you've changed, that you've quit drinking. But it isn't easy for me."

That he didn't mention sex was telling. He obviously didn't trust her about that either. Shivers of anxiety wracked her body. The cold, confused expression on his face chilled her. He'd always felt things deeply, but in the past he'd never had trouble making decisions. Was it her fault? Had she broken him?

She hopped up on her tiptoes and kissed him on the cheek. "Take some time. Think about it. When, or if, you decide to take a chance on me, let me know. You know where to find me."

He looked at her without speaking; his brows scrunched together, his arms crossed and his hands bunched into fists. There was a rigid fragility about him, and his eyes radiated hurt and confusion. Finally, he nodded.

"I'll think about it."

She kissed him again. "Do that. I'll be here when you make up your mind."

They stared at each other for several long minutes. His expression became increasingly unsure as their gazes clashed. With considerable effort, she kept her expression from changing. She kept it calm and sympathetic even though his uncertainty crushed what little hope she had left. After several moments, his face shuttered to blankness. He kissed her on the forehead and walked out of the shop.

She watched him go; each step he took carried him further away, crushing her hopes. When he turned the corner out of sight, she let the tears fall.

Chapter Nine

"Are you okay, Tea?" Willow's voice came from behind her.

"Of course she's not okay," Riley exclaimed. "He hurt her. Again."

Tea pivoted toward the voices. Moisture clouded her vision and she attempted a weak smile as a sob burst from her throat.

"Oh honey." They stepped forward in unison to hold her close until the tears trickled to a stop.

She sniffed loudly. "Okay, I'm done. How much did you hear?"

"Just the end. What happened before we arrived?" Riley asked.

"You wouldn't believe me if I told you." She tried for a laugh.

"Try us," Willow suggested.

Slowly, blowing her nose often, she explained the morning's argument and confessed to nearly making love to him by the creek.

"Holy crab apples," Willow exclaimed.

"You still love him? Don't you?" Riley asked.

Tea nodded. "I don't know why I let myself fall for him again."

"Again?" Willow asked. "It sounds like you never let him go."

"Yeah…"

"It has to be hard for him to see beyond the fact that you accidentally killed his mother," Riley said and poured them all coffee. They settled at a table in the corner. It was still dark outside as they sipped their ritual morning beverages. It was their habit to meet before work started a couple mornings a week. Sometimes Mandy Brighton joined them when she could escape her bakery.

"I know, but that doesn't make it any easier on me." Tea sighed. "I didn't know that she was drunk that night," Tea whispered. "He told me the other day that she was an alcoholic. In all those years, I never realized."

"That makes it worse for him I think," Riley said.

"I should have known better than to go hiking with him. I should have kept my distance. What was I thinking?"

Willow groaned. "Tea, what's going on with you? You aren't the self-pitying type. But you've been on this self-pity train for weeks. Get over yourself already." Her tone was teasing but there was underlying steel behind the words. The words weren't typical Willow. Usually she kept her opinions soft and gentle.

Today's harsh words jarred Tea. Willow was only coldly blunt when no other action worked. Great, now she'd pushed her friend too far.

"Fine," Tea spat out the word. "I'll get a grip. It's not like he's ever going to call again."

"He'll call," Willow asserted with Riley echoing her words.

"Sorry for being wrapped up in myself."

"Meditation might help," Willow advised. "It could help give you a new perspective."

"I'll try that. Enough about me," Tea said. "What's up with you, Willow? You've got a crazy glow about you."

"I have a date!"

Cheers and hugs erupted. When the revelry stopped, she continued her story.

"I went for groceries last night and I 'accidentally' bumped my cart into Sam Quinn's cart. I might have knocked the heck out of it, because his eggs hit the floor and exploded everywhere. We got to talking and he asked me out. We're having dinner tonight. What am I going to wear?" she moaned.

"What's that?" Tea asked, laughing. "You're never nervous or self-conscious."

"Crazy, right? But he's H-O-T! I mean I've always admired him, but when he touched me the electricity almost knocked my panties off."

They chuckled together.

"Seriously, I can't screw this up. I need to do it right."

"He'll love you. You've got nothing to worry about," Riley advised.

"Be yourself. That's all you should ever do." Tea patted Willow's hand. "Either he likes you or he doesn't. No sense in worrying about it. And wear that red dress, the one with the hidden split up the side that flashes your thigh when you move the right way."

"That's perfect!" Riley exclaimed. "I saw it when you wore it last Christmas."

"It's old!" Willow complained.

"Maybe, but it's so sexy, his jaw will drop and he'll smother you with drool," Tea giggled.

"There's an appealing image," Willow drawled. "But you're right. It'll be perfect."

They talked for half an hour, sipping coffee while Tea baked cookies and prepped the shop for opening. Eventually, Tea relaxed and managed to push Logan from her mind, sort of.

Chapter Ten

Two days later, Logan stormed into the firehall, oblivious to the rising sun and the early morning warmth of the last days of summer. In the mountains, the end of September could be freezing cold, or blisteringly hot.

"Wow, who crapped in your cereal?" Sam greeted him.

"Not talking about it," Logan snapped at his friend and supervisor. "It's none of your business."

"So, Chastity then? You've been on edge since you took her on that hike. I know you guys have history. That's the beauty of a small town, eventually everyone learns your secrets, even relative newcomers like me. I've only been here for four years, but I've heard all about you guys. Frankly, I was surprised when you asked her out."

"Yeah, me too," Logan confessed, hanging his jacket in his locker.

"So what did she do now?"

"Not going to talk about it." He slammed the locker shut.

"Okay, what did you do?"

"Cut a guy some slack, will you? What happened to the guy code?"

"It went out the window when I dumped on you when I found out my girlfriend had been cheating on me. Long distance relationships suck." Sam glared at Logan.

"So do short distance ones."

Operating by rote, they entered the parking bay to check the supplies on the trucks. They worked well in unison, carrying out a conversation and asking for items without breaking the flow of the chatter.

"She won't sleep with me," Logan blurted after making sure none of the other firefighters were within earshot.

"Why not?" Sam exclaimed, dropping a box of bandages on the floor.

"Because we don't have a relationship," Logan growled.

"So let me get this straight." Sam scooped up the bandages and tossed them back in the box, checking each package for damage. He tossed the box on a counter. "You're dating as kids, shit happened, you break up and don't speak for years. She has a fire in her shop and you play hero and help clean it up. You date a couple times and she won't sleep with you? Did she dump you?"

"Yes. No. She didn't ditch me."

"And is that all she is to you? A sex-buddy? From this side, it seemed like your relationship might get serious."

"It's complicated."

Sam's chuckle morphed into a full out laugh. "Now you sound like a chick."

"Stuff it." Logan slammed a compartment closed and wrenched the next one open.

"She killed my mom."

"On purpose?" Sam exclaimed.

"They were both drunk driving. Mom died. So did Corrie, Tea's best friend, but Tea survived." He struggled to keep the emotion from his voice.

"Was the accident dual fault? Or just Tea's?"

"Hell if I know," Logan growled, wondering what Sam was driving at.

"So maybe cut her some slack, she wasn't the only guilty party that night. By the sound of it neither one of them should have been on the road."

"How can I cut her slack? I'm so pissed off."

"Have you told her how you feel?"

"It's none of her business. I need two slings."

Sam tossed him the slings and Logan stuffed them into the bin.

"It is her business if you're going to date her."

"I don't want to date her."

"You just want to screw her?"

"I know what you're doing, playing devil's advocate. You pull that BS all the time. It doesn't work with me."

"And…"

"I think I still have feelings for her. After the other day, I thought sleeping with her again might end that. You know, take the pressure off so I can stop wondering. But she won't have sex."

Sam chuckled.

"It's not funny. I can't trust her long term. My mother's problems showed me that you couldn't trust an alcoholic. Who wants to leave their kids with a drunk? Hell, she probably wouldn't stay sober while she was pregnant."

"So you want her to have your babies?"

"I didn't say that." He snapped the first aid kit closed and opened the next one. He didn't say anything for several minutes as he sorted through the kit. "I don't know what I want."

"I think you want to see if you can trust her. She's been dry since I moved here. I've never seen her drink. Maybe it's true that she has a handle on her drinking. I know she didn't drink after the fire and you'd think that'd drive you to drink."

Sam paused and looked at Logan. "Is it Tea you're angry with, or your mother?"

The words were like a sucker-punch to the gut.

Logan grunted noncommittally. *He wasn't angry with his mother too, was he?*

"Think about it. And for what it's worth, I think you should risk it. Have a few dates. Maybe some laughs. See where it goes. Only time will prove if she's sober and if you can trust her."

"That's what she said."

"I guess you know what you have to do then."

"Hmph."

Chapter Eleven

She was back.

Tea watched the scruffy young girl sneak through the front door of The Tea Shop behind Dan O'Leary. Dan was a regular at the shop and could always be easily swayed to try something new. He was Tea's favorite victim for testing new coffee or cookie recipes on because she could count on him to give a forthright and honest opinion every time. The girl slipped around Dan and glancing wearily around as if being sure she wasn't spotted, headed toward the washrooms at the back of the shop. She had a skittish scared look about her that set alarm bells ringing in Tea's brain.

Beneath her ragged sweater and loose men's shirt, the girl's belly bulged suspiciously. What was she hiding? She lugged a heavy canvas bag and peeked shiftily at the other patrons as she went by. Her reddish-brown hair hung in long lank strands, clinging to her back. Her ragged jeans sported several stains and damp marks, their legs dragged against the floor leaving wet smudges. Tea watched her sidle out of view and into the short hallway.

The girl was attractive beneath the dirt; she had the air of a street person. She was young for that. Perhaps she was a runaway. What terror would cause someone so young and pretty to take to the streets? The alarm bells clanged louder.

"Watch the front for me, please, Willow. I have something I need to check on." She nodded toward the back as she addressed her friend and employee.

Willow's blue eyes followed Tea's glance. "Good idea. She's upset. Be careful, don't spook her."

Tea gathered some supplies from the janitorial closet and slipped into the ladies' room.

The young girl whirled around guiltily, her eyes wide with fright, her hands dripping water.

"Oh, I'm sorry," Tea apologized. "I didn't know anyone was in here. Do you mind if I refresh some supplies while you finish up?" She busied herself filling the paper towel and soap dispensers.

The girl's eyes darted back and forth before she cautiously resumed washing.

"Welcome to The Tea Shop. I'm Tea. That's short for Chastity." She introduced herself.

"Um. Hi."

"It's a beautiful day for mid-September. I wish I was outside instead of stuck inside working."

"It's nice out, but I miss my job," the girl blurted.

"Oh, what did you do?" If Tea could keep her talking, maybe she'd lose the scared rabbit look and relax.

"I worked in a book store. I miss the books."

"Are you a reader?"

"Ya, mostly ones about wizards and magic, like *Harry Potter*. And dragons. I love dragons." Her tone was wistful and sad.

"Oh, like Anne McCaffrey? I love her work." Tea watched the stiffness ease in her guest's shoulders. Perhaps she was making some headway in discovering the truth about her enigmatic visitor.

"Me too." She offered a shy smile. "But my parents' didn't like me reading that stuff." The tension returned two-fold.

"That's too bad. If you like dragons and magic, you should talk to Willow, out front. She's a self-proclaimed expert on the subject."

The girl's eyes glowed with interest for a second before an emotionless blank shuttered them. "I can't stay. I came in to use the washroom. That's okay, isn't it?" She fidgeted on her feet and glanced past Tea toward the door.

"Absolutely. Have you got time for tea?" Tea's heart softened another notch. The girl was shaking like a leaf in a windstorm. She was terrified.

"Um, I can't afford anything today. Maybe another day?" she said wistfully.

"How about I buy you a cup?"

"Um. No thanks." She edged toward the exit.

"My treat. You can repay me by buying a cup for someone else when you can afford it. Think of it as a random act of kindness. Pass it on when you're able."

"Why?"

"Why what?" Tea smiled kindly, trying to ease her distress.

"Why buy me tea? What do you want from me? Are you just keeping me here until the cops show up?" Her harsh words carried more fear than anger.

"Goodness, why would I do that? I'll be honest with you...you're exhausted, and a bit nervous. I've been there and it sucks." That was the understatement of the year. "Why don't we go out front and have tea together. Like friends."

Emotions marched across the girl's face: anxiety, need, reluctance and finally a glimmer of hope. "Okay. I guess. But I can't stay long. I have places to go." Her words were heavy with mock defiance and self-importance.

Tea's heart ached at the sorrow and fear on the young girl's face. "Come on then..." She paused waiting for the girl to supply her name.

"Destiny."

"Come on then, Destiny. Let's have a cup of tea and a visit. Finish washing up and I'll meet you out front." She smiled reassuringly and walked out of the bathroom. Tea waited at the counter talking to Willow. Destiny finally came out after enough time passed that Tea was debating going to check on her.

"Willow, this is my friend, Destiny. We're going to sit over there, near the back. Can you bring us a pot of tea and oatmeal raisin cookies?"

"You've got it boss. What kind of tea?" She flashed a glance at Destiny's belly.

What was she trying to say?

"Do you have a preference, Destiny?" Willow asked. "We have everything. I'm partial to lemon myself,"

"Not really. Anything's good." She stared at the floor and shuffled her feet nervously. "No caffeine. It keeps me awake."

"You heard the lady, Willow. Something without caffeine, please." She touched Destiny lightly on the shoulder. "Come sit. Take a load off your feet." Tea took a step forward and turned back to reassure Destiny.

The girl's stomach bulged distinctively against her shirt. Oh butternut! That's what Willow was hinting at. How did a girl this young end up pregnant and on the street? Was her pregnancy the cause of her being on the street or the result of it? Tea didn't have the answer to any of those questions, but it was obvious that Destiny needed help.

Sliding into a chair, she flashed another smile. "It's good to be off my feet. It's barely mid-morning, but I'm tired already. I guess being crazy busy yesterday did a number on them."

She struggled to remain calm and not blurt out the myriad of questions running rampant in her brain. Willow would say that fate had lead Destiny into the shop for a reason. Hadn't she been babbling on earlier about a stranger needing help? Sometimes having a semi-psychic friend was a mixed blessing.

Destiny perched uneasily on the edge of her chair, her hands clenched tightly in her lap. Her uneasy demeanor radiated fear and mistrust. She must be starving to accept the offer of tea and cookies in spite of that fear.

"Here you go camomile-lemon tea." Willow slid a tray onto the table. There were cookies, tea, two muffins and a sliced up orange on the tray. "Bon appetit." With her face turned so Destiny couldn't see, Willow gave Tea a warning glance.

Was she kidding? Did she really think that Tea was oblivious to the tension here?

Tea set the cups on the table and decanted the tea. "Help yourself to a snack," she said picking up a cookie and biting into it.

Destiny snatched up a cookie and gobbled it down as if she were afraid someone would take it away before she finished.

"Relax, Destiny. You're safe here. I don't know what you're running from. Or who. Nevertheless, you can relax here. You're not in any danger, nor is your baby."

Destiny choked on the last crumbs of her cookie and jerked to her feet.

Grasping her hand lightly, Tea urged her to take her seat. "I said you're safe. You don't have to share your story. We don't have to talk. Take a breather. Sit for a while. When you're ready, you can go. Tea's on the house, so are the snacks."

Destiny relaxed infinitesimally. "Why?"

"I think we covered this already. Random act of kindness. You're in a rough spot; I'm in a good one. Someday the tables will turn and you can repay me by helping someone else out."

Destiny nodded warily.

Anger spiked up Tea's spine. Not at Destiny, but at the person, or people who put this young girl into a place where she was running scared from everyone. Nobody deserved to live like this, no matter what. Somehow, she was certain that Destiny hadn't done anything wrong.

They sat in silence for a long time, sipping tea. Destiny finished off all the food on the tray while Tea watched. The young pregnant girl relaxed bit by bit. Finally, with everything consumed, she stood and smiled at Tea.

"I don't know why you did this, but thank you. I have to go."

"There's no need to rush off."

"Thanks." She turned and stepped away.

"Destiny," Tea called softly and waited until she turned around to finish her thought aloud. "If you ever need anything, please come back. I'm always here. If not, I live upstairs."

Logan entered the shop as Destiny exited. He ambled up to Tea and glanced back and forth from her to the door.

"How do you know that girl? She was with Mr. Zed when he reported the fire," he informed Tea.

She slid behind the counter to resume work.

"That's Destiny. She's the girl I told you about the night of the fire. I think she's homeless. I caught her in the bathroom. I managed to get some food into her before she took off. I think she might be in trouble of some sort. I'm worried about her." There was a lot more to Destiny's story than she had mentioned, not that the teenager had said very much.

"Maybe we should get Roger Nallos to look into it. The RCMP would know if she was missing. Is she pregnant?"

Tea knew him well enough to understand the tone of his voice indicated concern rather than censure.

"I'm pretty sure she is, judging by the bulge under her shirt and that she avoided caffeine. How does something like that happen?" She shook her head sadly. "You're right though, I'll talk to Roger when he stops in. He's in almost every shift."

"Isn't it cops and donuts?" Logan chuckled.

"It seems Roger has a thing for my chocolate chip cookies. And a double shot espresso with three sugars. His partner, who's a total strong-and-black-coffee guy, rides him about it all the time."

They laughed together.

Logan cleared his throat.

"Did you want to get some dinner tonight? I was thinking that we could order Chinese and watch a movie at my place."

Tea glanced at him, surprised by the question. "Like a date?"

He glanced at the floor before responding. "Yeah."

"Are you sure?" she asked him. He seemed...off kilter.

"No." He flashed a self-deprecating grin. "Not remotely."

"Then why?"

"Because the only way to determine if I can forgive you is to spend time with you." He glanced away, refusing to meet her gaze.

Ouch. That hurt. Conflicting thoughts chased each other through her head. He wanted to trust her, which was good and bad. He wanted to date her, which was good. Maybe. Should she want to take a chance on him, on being wounded again when she failed to live up to his expectations?

"It's okay," he said quietly. "You don't have to."

"What?'

"I get it. You don't want to."

"No. Actually I do. Is seven okay?" Perversely, she liked that he was nervous and willing to back down if she wasn't sure.

"Seven will be perfect. Do you want me to pick you up?"

"I'll walk."

"I'll order lemon chicken, assuming you still love it."

"It's still my favorite," she agreed.

"Your order's ready." Willow set two trays of coffee and a paper bag on the counter by the cash register.

"Thanks, Willow." Logan and Tea moved past the display case. He leaned over the counter and tugged on a lock of Tea's hair. "I'll see you later." He paid for his order, scooped it up and disappeared out the front door.

Chapter Twelve

Tea paused at the end of the sidewalk leading up to Logan's front step. The house hadn't changed much. He'd painted the formerly green bungalow steel grey and added an attached garage to one end. The white trim was pristine. The late fall flowers were a surprise. They were annuals too, not perennials. She hadn't realized that he kept the gardens up. They'd been his mother's pride and joy. He'd mowed the lawn and lights shone in the curtained windows. A shadow passed by the front window, behind the sheers.

Logan. Waiting for her.

She hurried up the walk and he jerked the door open before she could knock.

"Whoa!" she exclaimed.

"Sorry. I thought you were debating leaving. I didn't want you to."

"Honestly, it did cross my mind."

He winced.

She giggled nervously. "I decided to stay, to give you, to give us, a chance."

"I guess I deserved that."

It was her turn to grimace. "Actually, you didn't." She stuck out her hand. "Let's start again. Hi, I'm Chastity Howell, call me Tea."

He lifted one brow questioningly and then it morphed into a full-fledged smile.

"Nice to meet you." He took her hand and shook it warmly. "I'm Logan Wright. Please, come in."

"Thank you," she replied formally, stepping over the threshold into the house and slipping out of her jacket. She took a moment to study him while he hung up her coat. His face was still slightly damp from shaving and he smelled of toothpaste and citrusy cologne. Yummy. His perfectly pressed, navy and white checked shirt tucked neatly into his jeans. He was barefoot; his toenails cut short and neat. She liked that. She'd dated a few men who missed small grooming details and discovered that they often skimped on more important hygiene rituals. Yuck.

Tearing her gaze away from him, she glanced around. "Oh, it looks so different. I like it." She slipped out of her black suede walking boots and strode through the small foyer into the living room.

"I love the leather," she exclaimed, stroking the back of an oversized brown leather couch that sat kitty-corner to a well-used matching recliner. "Are those the tables your grandfather made?"

"They are. I refinished them last year. They were beat to crap. James, Julia and I were pretty hard on them. We trashed a lot of furniture. It's a wonder my folks didn't kill us."

"I remember. We broke the leg off the kitchen table that time...what were we doing?"

"Theoretically speaking, we were making pizza. In reality, it was a full on food fight."

"Man, that was a blast."

"Until Dad got home. You and I got in such trouble we were supposed to be watching the twins."

"I remember. Your dad said, 'You two are two years older than the twins. I expect you to be responsible and take care of them and to show them how to behave.' Gosh, how many times did we get that lecture? Hundreds?" She chuckled.

"At least. I talked to them last night. James is exhausted; internship and medical rounds are kicking his butt. Julia is engaged to a dentist in the office she's going to work for when she's finally finished school. Sometimes I feel like I let my folks down not becoming a doctor or dentist," he confessed abruptly.

"What? Are you nuts? You're a fireman! You save hundreds of lives a year and keep the whole town safe. Your dad must be proud of you."

"He says he is, but occasionally I wonder..."

"Don't be silly." She mock-slapped his arm. "You know he'd tell you if he wasn't. We can't all be doctors. Look at me, I'm a glorified cashier and I don't sweat over it."

"You're the owner of a successful tea shop. You have a good solid business and you make the best cookies."

"And I love it," she confessed. "I wouldn't be happy doing anything else. I like to think that Gran would be proud if she looked down on me."

"I know she would be. She loved that teashop, and you."

"Look at us." She laughed. "We're a mutual admiration society."

He grinned just as the doorbell rang.

"Oh, that'll be the food." He left her standing in the living room, wrapped in memories and went to retrieve their supper.

"Come into the kitchen," he said returning from the door. "I've made a few changes."

"Wow!" she exclaimed stepping into what was once a small functional room. "It's huge. And look at the marble countertops."

"You're drooling," he teased. "I knocked the back wall out and extended it twelve feet. I have forty linear feet of countertop a walk-in pantry with an upright freezer. You could cook for fifty people here without trouble."

"I love the mahogany cupboards," she said as he extracted containers from a take-out bag. "Those handles are simple but elegant. Oh, my gosh! Look at that backsplash." She wandered up to the counter and stroked the multi-colored stones. Are these your dad's gemstones?"

"It took us two months to cut and polish enough of the rocks we collected over the years. Then we had to glue them and grout them." He touched one close to her hand. "This one is part of that petrified wood chunk you found when you came to Oregon with us that summer you were twelve."

"I remember that." She pretended to pry it from the wall. "Give me back my rock."

"The rest of it is in the garage." He laughed. "But we couldn't resist putting a couple slices of it in here." He pointed out a few spectacular specimens. There was rose quartz, goldstone, jade, amethyst, several colors of jasper and agate. There were even a few small pieces of amber included.

"This is gorgeous. You know that you can never sell this house, right? How could you ever part with this?" She waved toward the backsplash.

"I have no intention of selling this house. I grew up here. There are so many memories. Good and bad." He looked sad for a moment. "I've updated, renovated, insulated...the list is endless."

"You've done a wonderful job. But you missed one thing."

"What's that?" He looked around as if trying to catch what he'd forgotten.

"You forgot to feed me," she teased. "I'm ravenous."

"Help yourself." He handed her a plate. "Would you like a glass of wine?"

"No thanks," she replied lightly even as she wondered if this were a test. "Since we just met," she said referring to their earlier mock-introduction, "you should know that I'm a recovering alcoholic. However, I would love some ice water."

"Crap. I didn't mean to…"

"Relax, Logan. You don't have to walk on eggshells around me. People drink. It doesn't bother me. Well, not most of the time. I can deal with it."

He opened his mouth, closed it again and groaned. "Sorry. Ice water it is." He poured them both generous glasses. "Shall we eat here or while we watch TV?"

"Oh, TV definitely. I saw that television. What is it, forty-six inches?"

"Sixty," he said proudly.

"Compensating for something?" she teased, knowing he wasn't.

"Well," he drawled. "A man's television should match the size of his...kitchen." He laughed when she choked on her water.

"Jerk."

"Never, ever, tease a man about the size of his…television."

A soft thump sounded on the back door.

Logan strolled over to it and opened it. A large white dog wiggled in and sat patiently on the mat.

"Good boy." He patted the dog on the head. "Max, this is the woman I told you about. This is Tea. She's my friend. Friend," he repeated. Max looked up at him and Logan nodded.

Having received permission, Max walked over to sit at Tea's feet, his tail wagging as he waited for her attention.

"Can I pet him?" She wasn't afraid, she was cautious.

"Sure, he loves people. He's a white German Shephard and he lacks a little in the manners department," he added when Max let go a soft, impatient bark.

Tea kneeled and let Max smell her hand before she scratched him between the ears. "Who's a good boy?" Max leaned into her touch and then rolled over so she could scratch his belly.

"Really, Max? Submissive? After one stroke? Dog, women are going to be the death of you," Logan joked. "You're supposed to be a tough search and rescue dog, not a wimp."

"Don't listen to the big mean man. You're not a wimp. You're wonderful," Tea said in a baby talk voice and tickled Max's belly. "He's adorable," she said, looking up at Logan. "Can he watch TV with us?"

"Some date this is turning out to be," Logan complained.

Beneath the gruff words, Tea read his pleasure that both dog and woman had passed approval.

They sat alongside one another on the couch. Close, but not quite touching. Max, however had no such reservations and settled on the floor, his nose resting on Tea's knee.

"What would you like to watch? I have a ton of DVDs or Netflix, no cable."

"Oh, *Goonies* is on Netflix."

"*Goonies*? That must be a thousand years old."

"Not quite," she chortled. "I still love it. I remember when we saw it at the drive-in."

"Classic movie week," he chuckled.

"Do you mind?" she asked.

"At your command, you Goonie."

"Thanks," she replied simply. "Gran and I must have watched it a dozen times. That and *Indiana Jones*. Gosh, she loved Harrison Ford."

"I'm pretty sure you had a thing for him too," Logan teased.

"At least I didn't have the hots for Princess Leia and her tinfoil bikini."

"I'm a lot older now and I still think that GOLD bikini was hot. She was a bit skinny for my tastes. I like a little...cushioning." He turned away.

"Oh my gosh. I can't believe you said that, on our first date."

"I can't believe it either." The pink flush in his cheeks deepened to red, but he leaned in and shoulder bumped her companionably and then shoveled in a huge mouthful of rice.

"I'll let it go this time."

"Thanks," he mumbled around his food.

"And don't talk with food in your mouth," she chided.

"Yes, ma'am," he said with his mouth full.

"Oh you." She patted his thigh and chuckled. Weird how she couldn't keep her hands off him.

They fell into a companionable silence as the movie started. It was like old times when they could sit together silently and not worry what the other was thinking. They laughed in all the places they'd enjoyed in the past and fell into quiet, meaningless conversation, watching and talking at the same time.

"Did you want to watch something else?" he asked as the movie ended.

"Zombies?"

"Really? You like zombies?"

"No...I love zombies. Best movies ever. *Shaun of the Dead*. Please."

He groaned and got up to locate the DVD on the shelf.

"You actually have it?"

"I love zombie movies. Would you mind clearing the dishes and refilling our drinks while I get this started?"

"As you wish." She gathered the plates and carried them to the kitchen. Closing her eyes, she took a moment to savor the warm, comfortable feeling she had when she was with him. It was so much like old times, but with an undercurrent of tension. It wasn't just 'getting to know him' tension; there was a walloping dose of sexual tension.

Puffing out a calming breath, she refilled their glasses and returned to the living room. She handed him his and settled beside him on the couch, close enough to feel the heat of his body without touching him. She was already in dangerous territory, but there was no sense in pushing her resolve too far.

Chapter Thirteen

Debilitating muscle cramps plagued Logan's right arm. His fingers had passed cramped twenty minutes ago. He'd lost all sensation. Pleasant as it was having Tea in his arms, Logan had to disturb her rest, even if it destroyed the perfect view he had of her cleavage. A man could get lost there…

"Hey, wake up." He nudged her in the shoulder. She grunted and snuggled closer to him. Her breast pushed up against his arm and he felt an involuntary hardening in his jeans.

He did not need this. She'd fallen asleep against him about ten minutes after the movie started and his arm was numb. He didn't want to wake her up but he couldn't sit here like this any longer. And if she slid any further forward, she'd end up with her face in his lap. He stiffened further.

Damn.

"Chastity, honey? Wake up. The movie's over. Time to get up. Tea?"

She grunted and turned her face up to nuzzle his chin.

"Chastity," he said harshly.

She leaned back and smiled sleepily at him. "Hmm. I was having such a good dream."

"You were smiling and moaning in your sleep," he teased.

She bolted upright. "I was not."

"Yes, you were." He chucked her under the chin, making no effort to hide his amusement. Teasing her kept her attention on his face and far from his groin. Not that she wanted anything to do with that part of him. He bit back a disappointed sigh. She might not want to go there, but he sure did.

"Come on, girl, I'll drive you home."

"I can walk," she disagreed sleepily.

"It's late and it snowed a skiff."

"All the more reason for you to stay here; the roads and sidewalks will be slippery. I'll stick to the grass and I'll be fine. I'll text you when I get home." Gathering up their glasses, she strolled into the kitchen, working the kinks out of her shoulders as she went. "How long was I asleep?"

"You slept through the entire zombie apocalypse."

"Dang, I missed it." She chuckled and loaded the tumblers into the dishwasher.

Logan would hand wash their dishes once she left. He used so few dishes it wasn't worth the water or energy to run the blasted thing. Sometimes he wondered why he'd created such a fabulous kitchen. Lord knows he spent very little time there and rarely cooked. He was more likely to use the enormous stainless steel barbeque on the back deck than he was to use the oven.

At the front door, Max sat and stared adoringly up at Tea as she shrugged into her jacket. Logan reached for his.

Tea placed a restraining hand on his arm. "Stay. I walk all the time. I'll be fine. Max, you keep him here." She laughed when the dog grinned back at her and stepped in front of Logan. "See, even Max knows I'm right."

"And I know when I'm defeated. Thank you for a lovely evening."

"Sorry I dozed off on you. It's been a long week for me. Things have settled down since the fire, but everything is back in order, including Willow's room.

Tonight was a lovely evening. Good company and good food."

"You devoured that lemon chicken and the ginger beef too. I thought you were going to bite my hand off," he teased.

"Never get in between me and my food," she joked back. "Goodnight, Logan." She ruffled Max's fur. "I'll text when I get home."

Logan followed her outside and stood watching her walk away. Just before she stepped around the corner out of sight, she turned and gave him a small wave. He reciprocated, pleased that she looked back.

Why had she turned? Was she checking to see if he was watching her? Was she wondering why he hadn't kissed her? Did she want him to or would she have raced out the door if he tried? Would she understand that he was trying not to push her into a physical relationship, in spite of wanting one?

How could one woman confuse him this badly?

Chapter Fourteen

"So, how was it?" Cynthia asked when she showed up for work the next day.

"How was what?"

"Your date with Logan." She smirked.

"I'm not dating Logan," Tea denied, extracting a baking sheet from the oven.

"Oh, those smell good."

"Lemon sugar cookies. It's a recipe from an old friend." Cynthia reached for one. "At least let them cool," Tea chided.

"Okay, but only if you tell me about your date." Her eyes sparkled with mischief.

"What date?"

"I saw you leave his house last night. He stood on the step and watched until you went around the corner."

"You're spying on me? I'm your boss," she chided gently

Cynthia giggled. "No way! I live across the street. I was going to bed after cramming for my physics test. I looked out the window and there you were. So, how was your date?"

"Who went on a date?" Willow asked, coming out of her room with Riley hot on her heels.

"There was no date!" Tea exclaimed. Good gravy, a woman couldn't get a break around here for anything, and she was the boss.

"She was at Logan's last night," Cynthia tattled.

Tea blushed, torn between annoyance and exasperation. "It wasn't a date, exactly."

"So what was it?" Mandy Brighton chimed in as she strode up to the counter. Her brown eyes flashed and she tossed her highlighted hair over her shoulder.

"Mandy, hi." Tea greeted her with enthusiasm. "What brings you here this time of day?"

"You mean besides wanting to hear about your date?" she joked. "Kelsey accidentally dropped my last bottle of vanilla and broke it. I was shorted on my order last week, so I'm all out until tomorrow. I could go to the grocery store, but I thought you might be able to spare me some…after you give us the lowdown on your date."

"There. Was. No. Date!" Tea exclaimed.

"It wasn't a date?" Logan chimed in.

"Oh. Ah. Gah. What is this place? Gossip central?" Amused frustration ratcheted up her spine. There was no privacy in this town.

"It wasn't a date?" Logan repeated himself, laughing lightly.

Tea sighed. "Fine. Okay. It was a date. But what we did and how it went is none of your business." She pinned each woman with a glare.

Logan put his hand in front of his mouth and loudly whispered, "It was fabulous."

Everyone battered him with questions.

"Butternut!" Tea cursed.

"No details here," he hedged. "I think I've dug myself in deep enough already. No sense pouring more gas on the fire." He chuckled. Moving around the counter he gathered Tea into his embrace. "Hi," he said simply and kissed her on the forehead.

Cynthia sighed blissfully.

"Can I get that vanilla before you forget?" Mandy teased.

Tea handed her the vanilla. "Replace it when you have a chance, I've got lots."

Mandy thanked her and headed back to her bakery. Tea called out after her, "You owe me a cupcake."

"You've got it."

"Cynthia, can you start clearing tables? I was swamped for a while and didn't get to them. And you guys," she said glaring at Willow and Riley. "You guys can keep your speculations to yourself. Now go, shoo." She waved them away.

"What can I do for you, Logan?" She smiled warmly at him once everyone had cleared out.

"I came to ask you to dinner."

"We had dinner last night." She deflected the question. He was confusing her again. Last night's date had been nice, but just days ago he wanted nothing to do with her. Part of her was thrilled, the rest was...cautious.

"Don't you eat every night?" he asked. "I know I do."

"Logan..." She tried to keep the confusion and impatience from her voice but she missed the mark.

"What is it, Tea?"

"I don't know. It's..." He was moving too fast. She couldn't deal with his abrupt direction changes.

"Technically, I haven't changed directions since last night. I asked you out, you accepted and now I'm asking you again."

"I said that out loud?" She winced. "Fudge."

He smirked. "You did. So, can I buy you dinner?"

She pondered it for a moment. "I'll make you dinner instead. My place, seven-thirty?"

"Six-thirty," he countered. "I've got a staff meeting at eight."

"Fine," she agreed grudgingly.

"Whoa, slow down. Bank that enthusiasm before it gets out of hand."

"I'm being a cow, aren't I?" She didn't mean to be, she just couldn't help herself. In spite of their lovely evening the night before, he still left her unbalanced.

"A bit," he teased. "But I like beef."

It took a second for the joke to sink in. She groaned at his bad word play. "You'd think you'd get better jokes."

His rogue grin turned serious. "Honestly, Chastity. You leave me unbalanced too. I'm not sure how to deal with it. We have such a checkered past and I have issues. I'm not trying to force this. However, after thinking about what you said the other day, I decided that you're right. The best way for me to learn to trust you is to spend time with you."

He cracked his knuckles and she winced.

"Sorry, I forgot you hate that. Please have dinner with me," he asked quietly.

"I will. See you at six-thirty. And I'm only agreeing because Cynthia is working tonight."

"What? It wasn't my charming personality or my handsome good looks?"

"You never quit, do you?" She laughed at his mock exasperation.

"Not when I see something I want." He kissed her on the head and disappeared out the back door.

***

She heard him jog up the stairs and knock on the door to her suite.

"Come in," she called out happily, unable to keep the smile from her voice.

He let himself in while she drained the pasta and added the meat sauce. Stirring it together, she ladled it into two small casserole dishes and layered it with cheese.

"Is that double cheese baked spaghetti?" He asked.

"Wipe your lip," she teased. "You're drooling."

"Over you, not the food. You look nice."

"She looked down at herself. Black jeans, with a white blouse and cardigan, it wasn't fancy by far, especially with an apron covering most of it.

"I've got my back to you," she countered. "You can't even see me."

"I like what I see." He patted her butt and kissed the top of her head.

She shook her head and slid out of his reach.

"No touching."

"You're in a better mood." He held out a bouquet of carnations.

She slid the dishes into the oven for the final bake and accepted the flowers. She buried her face in them and inhaled deeply. "Mm, I love carnations. And pink ones too. You remembered."

"I did. Carnations and tiger lilies are your favorite. Did you think I'd forget?" He cast a questioning look at her.

"I never really considered it. This is all happening so fast. I'm having trouble keeping up, and keeping my balance. Sometimes I feel like I'm waiting for the other shoe to drop."

"Ouch." He winced.

"I didn't mean it like that." She started spreading herbed butter on a loaf of French bread. "It's like this..." She paused to gather her thoughts.

"I'm not who I was, and neither are you. But I can't help but expect things to be the way they were. Before it got ugly. I know that's not a reasonable expectation, but that's how it is. I'm finding it hard to adapt. We were so close for so long, and then we were virtual enemies. Now, we're somewhere in between. I feel like I'm floundering in an ocean of uncertainty and can't find the shore. I don't know what to expect and that bothers me."

"You don't pull any punches do you?" he asked seriously.

"I can't. There's too much water under the bridge and there's more rushing in. I'm just trying to stay afloat. Can you understand that?"

He gripped her upper arms gently in his hands and looked her right in the eye. He didn't say anything; he studied her. Several emotions washed over his face. Anticipation, need, tenderness and finally fear and confusion.

"I get it," he said at last. "I couldn't forgive you and I couldn't stop the destructive path you were on. You were a train wreck. I couldn't watch it either. Unfortunately, walking away didn't help. In a town this size, there's no escaping your past. Your grandmother asked me to take part in your intervention. I wouldn't; I couldn't. Nobody, ever, not even my own parents, has given me hell like that. She would barely speak to me for years, not until I went to your grandfather's funeral." He dropped his hands and rubbed his palms on his jeans.

This wasn't easy for him, she realized. He was forcing the words out, opening up to her, maybe against his better judgement.

"If it makes a difference, she nagged me until she died, to talk to you, to try and make amends," Tea admitted.

"You did, you came to the house about two years after the intervention."

"Your dad said you wouldn't see me." Her voice was accusatory.

"I told him to. But I listened when you apologized to him, and hearing what you had to say, I wished I hadn't refused."

"You should have come out." She didn't understand his refusal then, and still didn't. "What would it have hurt to hear me out?"

"Then, it would have broken my heart, worse than it was. Mom's problems keep me from listening to you; that and my pride."

She snorted agreement.

"What I'm saying, I guess., is that I recognize your mixed feelings. Okay, I don't understand them, but I do see where you're coming from. I'm trying to get beyond my biases and accept you for who you are now."

"I'm trying too, but you had such hatred on for me for so long..." She trailed off.

"Not hatred, not exactly. I don't have the words for it." He turned away and paced the room. Stopping in front of her, he sighed. "I'm working on it, Chastity. For what it's worth I'm trying my best to forgive you, to put it into the past."

"Thank you," she whispered. She blinked away the tears that threatened to spill over. "I can't ask for more than that."

It was her turn to look away. She busied herself preparing the garlic bread and sliding it in the oven. While it toasted, they set the table.

"Spinach salad okay with you?" she asked when she finally found her voice.

He wrinkled his nose.

"Still the same old Logan, hating spinach?" She snickered, his sour expression lightening her mood.

"I'll try it."

"Whoa, the great Logan Wright is willing to try spinach? Stop the presses. Batten down the hatches. Alert the media," she teased.

"Hardy-har-har. You're a laugh a minute."

She placed a pile of precut ingredients and a bowl on the counter. "I've prepped everything, just put it in the bowl and toss it."

"Bacon? In salad?" he asked in disbelief as he surveyed the fixings. "And eggs? What are those little berry-looking things?"

"Um, berries?" She chuckled at his mock glare.

"It's a twist on classic spinach salad. Baby spinach, bacon, egg, dried strawberries, mushrooms and raspberry vinaigrette dressing. It's good for you, well except the bacon. You don't have to eat it. Although Gran would have made you at least taste it."

She sliced up the garlic loaf, nestled it beside the spaghetti on plates, and carried them to the table. "Will you bring the salad, please?"

He carried the salad over and placed it alongside the dressing she'd set there earlier.

"Are you chewing?"

He flushed guiltily. "Bacon," he mumbled around a mouthful.

"You're stealing my bacon?" she teased. "Bad, bad, Logan."

"You'll have to punish me."

She choked out a laugh at the double entendre and chortled outright when his face flushed.

"And he blushes too," she teased.

"Ha, ha, knock it off, funny girl." He joined her at the table and they shared small talk while eating.

"What was it you said about garlic and dates?" she asked.

"It makes your date wary of kissing you."

"Guess I'm safe for the night then."

"Maybe, but I had garlic too..." he trailed off to silence. "That was the best double-baked spaghetti I ever had. Gran's recipe?" Logan asked. "And what did you do to the bread?"

"Parmesan cheese and a hint of fetta, basil and garlic. It's more of herbed bread. Willow taught me that one."

"Maybe I'll have to ask her out. I do love a woman who can cook." He winked.

"You do that. But I think she has her eye on someone else." Tea knew he was joking. He'd never been the type to date more than one woman at a time.

"Darn, missed the boat on that one. And, I have to admit that spinach salad isn't that bad."

"I gathered that," she quipped, "since you ate three bowls of it."

"What can I say, I work hard and I need a lot of food. Speaking of work." He glanced at his watch. "I have to run or I'll be late for the staff meeting. Then two late nights and three days off, maybe we can do something together."

The cautious hesitancy in his voice charmed her.

"Perhaps we can. It'll depend on the weather and how busy the shop is."

"I can deal with that."

"Maybe I'll put you to work washing dishes if it's busy," she teased.

He looked aghast, making her laugh.

They cleared the table together, putting the dishes in the sink at her insistence. "I'll hand wash them later, I don't have a dishwasher. One person doesn't really need a dishwasher."

They walked to the door. He slid into his jacket and looked down at her. "You know, you aren't actually that short, maybe I'm just tall."

"You're a giant. You make me feel short."

"You fit well in my arms, you always did." He gathered her in his embrace and smiled at her.

Rising up on her tiptoes, she kissed him on the cheek. "Goodnight, Logan."

"Not good enough," he whispered and moved a fraction of an inch closer.

"Oh," she said, unsure if she was responding to his motion or his words.

"Oh, indeed. I'm going to kiss you goodnight. This is our third date; everyone kisses on the third date."

Tea did some quick mental calculations. "It's at least our fifth or sixth," she said with a grin.

"Does that include our dinner at Pasta Italia?" he whispered and moved in. "I'm sure I'm entitled to much more than a kiss."

She turned her face up and smiled. "I'll accept that, and grant you one kiss. Only one," she whispered, brushing her lips across his. Heat, light and arousal exploded across her skin. Her lips softened against his as he deepened the kiss.

His hands slid into her hair, holding her close as he pressed forward for more. She cupped the back of his head, drawing him down, her tongue battling with his. She stroked his back, exploring the solid plains of muscle and sinew. Such strength and power from his physical work.

Finally, she drew away. "Go." She gasped for breath.

"You like this, don't you?" There was a teasing lilt to his voice.

It wasn't really a question and she didn't answer as he tightened his grip in her hair and kissed her breathless again.

"Damn," he whispered when they came up for air. "I have to go." He brushed his lips across her temple and slipped out the door, closing it behind him.

"Bye," she called weakly and stumbled to the couch on wobbly legs. The man sure could kiss. If he'd stayed much longer, she'd have forgotten her vow not to sleep with him until she was sure he was in it for the long haul. Until she was certain this wasn't just a flash in the pan that would fizzle and burn out, she couldn't pander to her urges.

Chapter Fifteen

Eight-thirty the next evening, Tea wandered into the Thurston Hotel. She went past the valet stand and check-in desk to the lobby's sitting area. The lobby was brimming with excited women. Good grief, she'd almost been late to the party she'd organized. That's how it was when you had a decision-making disorder about what to wear. She studied the other members of the wedding party. Riley was stunning in an off the shoulder sheath of teal silk. Bailey Thurston wore a neat pantsuit with a pristine white blouse. Jade's outfit flashed with sparkles.

Beside them, Wendy, the wedding planner, Melanie Thurston, Kelsey, Charity and Riley's workmate and the bridesmaid, Amber Clarkson, were laughing and giggling together. This was going to be fabulous!

Tea had run the gamut from plain blue jeans to ones laden with bling. From there she'd gone to her new little black dress with the silver trim and heels. Finally, after several outfit changes, she settled on a sleek burgundy knit dress with a sparkly silver shawl and matching pumps. A little fancy for a casual dinner, but she loved dressing up and going out. During the week, she was your basic jeans and blouse girl, but for an evening out, she made every effort to impress. She'd straightened her brunette bob and tamed it into a degree of submission.

Riley hurried over to greet her. "Tea, I thought you'd never get here." They embraced warmly. "Wow, love those earrings!"

Tea shook her head, setting the strands of silver stars jingling and shining. "Thanks. I've had them for ages;

they seemed perfect for a celebration. Although, you should be the one wearing them, you're the star of the party tonight."

"Don't tell my mother that. She thinks I'm out for a quiet dinner with Brock. She'd pitch a fit if she discovered this was a bachelorette party."

"I can hear her now–'No daughter of mine would behave in *that* fashion.'" Tea impersonated Lilith Hamilton; characterizing her by raising her chin and pointing her nose in the air. The rest of the group hooted at the impression.

Someone proclaimed, "You captured her perfectly."

"I love my mother, but some days..." Riley didn't need to finish the sentence; everyone knew that Lilith Hamilton was a woman of strong opinions and never hesitated to let them be known. She'd been driving Riley crazy with her interpretation of the wedding plans. With the wedding scheduled for December, Riley's tension was ratcheting up and sometimes she commented that the best thing might just be to elope with Brock and save all the hassles.

That's what tonight was all about; blowing off some steam, relaxing and celebrating the upcoming nuptials. For a brief second, Tea was jealous of her friend's love life. She wished Riley every happiness but couldn't help but wish she'd find a way to end her own string of bad luck in love and find her own happily ever after. Maybe she'd get lucky and find her own Mr. Right. Right, not Wright. Although in the past couple weeks, she'd been getting along with Logan better than ever.

She shook her head to displace the thoughts that kept lodging there. This was a night of celebration.

"Let the party begin." She raised her fist in the air and headed toward Peaks Bar with her friends laughing along behind her.

The room was packed. It was a good thing they'd reserved a couple tables. Reservations weren't typical at the hotel bar, but Twyla Ingleheart, the bartender and manager, had accepted a reservation claiming that she knew a good thing when she saw it. A bachelorette party meant a lot of alcohol and appetizers consumed. Plus, the men would be out in force to drool over the ladies. Reserving them a table on a normally busy Friday night was good business.

They paraded in, past the mahogany bar where Twyla held court and into the middle of the room where two tables were together and labelled with a 'Reserved' sign. Raven-haired, feminine but still tough as nails, Twyla hustled over to take their drink orders. While the others ordered alcohol, Tea and Jade requested fruit juice coolers. A blend of fruit juice and club soda, it was visually indistinguishable from an alcoholic cocktail. When she first quit drinking, Tea had found that having coffee or tea at a party could make people uncomfortable. Her AA sponsor had suggested mocktails instead. It was a fabulous solution.

She'd learned to have fun without alcohol; being sober while her friends were a little buzzed didn't bother her as it once did. She loved being able to keep an eye on her friends and keep them out of trouble, the bonus being that the group always had a designated driver, even if she had to borrow one of their cars. When the drinks arrived, she took a long slow sniff of Amber's rye. She still craved the smell of alcohol.

They laughed and giggled, playing a ridiculous scavenger hunt, the object of which was to collect items from a list where each item had to be acquired without leaving the bar. They pestered other patrons, who joined in the fun willingly.

Deep in a conversation with Riley, who wore a mock veil decorated with the bows from her gifts, Tea stilled when a shiver ran down her back. She cast a wary glance over her shoulder toward the door.

Logan.

Sometimes she swore her body had a sixth sense where he was concerned. She felt his arrival without seeing him. What was he doing here?

Their gazes collided. Heat rose in her face and her heart lurched. They stared at each other for a moment. He nodded solemnly and wove his way through the room, pausing to talk to Twyla at the bar. Tea followed his progress to the pool tables where he joined Sam Quinn and a couple of their friends. She'd been so busy visiting that she hadn't even noticed Sam come in.

Good, Logan was meeting someone. He wasn't here to check up on her. She returned her attention to her friends.

"God, he's so hot," Kelsey exclaimed. "Too bad he doesn't date."

Riley laughed. "You're married and he's only got eyes for Tea. They've been a couple since Tea was ten. They just refuse to admit it."

"That is not true," Tea objected.

"That explains so much," Charity said with a giggle.

"Why don't you admit it and go for it," Riley teased. "You'd both be so much happier."

Everyone pounced on the teasing, giving Tea a good ribbing over the sad state of her love life. She played along with them, barely managing to hide the pain skewering her heart. She did love him, but she'd never admit it to her friends. Tonight, she refused to spare him another glance. They'd never let the subject drop if she did. Instead, she played along with the joking until her friends tired of it and turned the topic to something else.

"Time for a toast." Tea stood and raised her drink in the air. "To Riley, the bride, the woman we love and envy. May she and Brock live as long as they want to and want to as long as they live." Everyone laughed and Melanie, who sat beside Tea, wobbled in her chair, nearly knocking her over. Their mirth doubled.

Without warning, someone snatched Tea's glass out of her hand.

She whirled around to stare at the offender.

Logan, again.

"Give that back," she demanded.

"Are you drunk?" His glare burned a hole straight through her.

"What business is it of yours?"

"Are you drunk?" he repeated. "Jesus, Tea. I thought you quit drinking, that you were sober but you've been hiding your drinking all along. I should have known that it was too good to be true. The old Chas is back. I never should have trusted you. People don't change."

His words were razor blades slicing through her. He didn't even give her the benefit of the doubt. She never should have opened herself up to him again. Why couldn't she learn that love wasn't for her?

"You have no idea what you're talking about." She glared right back, disappointment darkening her heart. "Take a drink, try it for yourself."

"I don't need to try it. I can see from the way you're behaving that you're pissed to the gills." He slammed the drink on the table.

"What the hell is wrong with you?" she screeched. "I'm having fun with my friends." Fury clouded her vision.

She choked back a scream at his self-righteous, sanctimonious attitude.

"You're all as pissed as billy goats. Can't you go out and not get wasted?"

The room fell silent, and held its collective breath. This could get ugly. Around them, people began backing away. Riley's hand flew to her mouth, her eyes widened in shock.

"You're ruining Riley's celebration. Leave us…leave me, alone. What I do, or don't do is none of your business; just like it's none of my business that you were over there sucking back beer."

"I had two beer and I'm walking home, not that it's any of your damn business."

A hand clamped down on Tea's shoulder. Twyla wedged her way between Tea and Logan. Her stare and her ridged stance froze them in place.

"Stop this right now. You're causing a scene in my bar." She glared back and forth between them. "Nobody fights in here. Logan, get your ass out of here before I have you arrested for disturbing the peace."

"Me?" His hands fisted but he didn't move. Tea recognized that stance. He was beyond angry. He wouldn't act on it, that wasn't in his nature, but he was irate.

"You," Twyla confirmed. "You're sticking your nose into something that isn't any of your business and you're interrupting a perfectly fine party."

His mouth opened and slammed shut without saying anything. He shrugged Twyla's hand off his shoulder, gave Tea a disappointed glare and stormed out.

Silence reigned for several interminable moments until Twyla glared around the bar, skewering people with a look. "What are you people staring at? Mind your own business."

Chatter erupted double time. No one in their right mind argued with Twyla. An MMA fighter, she was stronger than she looked and could kick the ass of half the men in town, without breaking a sweat. She'd trained under Georges St-Pierre and knew a couple of the famous Gracie brothers personally. Nobody messed with Twyla Ingleheart. Ever.

"Carry on, ladies." She smiled and walked away.

None of the bridal party spoke or smiled. The celebratory mood was gone. They peered cautiously to Tea for guidance.

"Ignore Logan," Tea said, hiding the hurt in her heart. "He's got some kind of bee in his bonnet about drinking." She shrugged his hurtful attitude off. "He isn't worth our time or effort. Ignore him; I know I'm going to."

She picked up her glass again and proclaimed, "To Riley and Brock, may they party together forever."

The festivities resumed, a little subdued, and after a while, everyone but Chastity forgot Logan had ever been there. If she ever spoke to him again, which was unlikely, she'd tell him a thing or two about manners, selfishness and his craptacular attitude. He'd pulled some stupid stunts in his day, but this one took the cake.

Chapter Sixteen

Logan stormed out of Peaks Bar. Twyla had her freaking nerve, sticking her big nose into his business. Man, that really burned him. And Tea? She pissed him off royally. He'd believed her when she claimed she was dry, that she'd quit drinking. Wasn't she just a big fat liar?

He punched the hotel's stone facade as he walked.

"Damn it. That hurt." It did nothing to relieve his anger. Now his knuckles were bloody and painful.

"Hey, Logan. Lo." His friend and co-worker, Sam, hailed him from the front steps of the hotel. "Hold up, buddy."

Logan kept walking. He didn't want to talk about this.

Sam jogged to catch up. "Wait up, asshat. I have your jacket. It's cold enough to freeze the balls off a brass monkey out here."

Logan didn't miss a step.

"Holy crap, what's eating you?" Sam paused. "Besides Tea?"

"Isn't that enough?" Logan snarled. He trudged toward the street.

"She wasn't drinking, you know. I asked Twyla. She's in the bar a lot and never has alcohol. Not even near-beer."

"You're sticking up for her? Some friend you are."

"I am your friend." He grabbed Logan's shoulder and jerked him to a halt. They stood there, nose to nose, glaring at each other. "That's why I'm out here in the freezing cold instead of inside talking to that hot chick at

Riley's party. You're wrong and you need to admit it. Talk to her. I think you can work this out."

"It's none of your business," Logan snarled and jerked free of Sam's grip. "I trusted her one time too many...I'm done."

"It's not over or you wouldn't be so hung up on it. If you care for her, you need to tell her."

"That's just it. I don't care about her anymore. I stopped caring about Chastity Howell when she started binge drinking and dropped out of high school. I hoped she'd changed, but she hasn't. She's the same old Chas and she's nothing to me anymore. Give it a rest."

"Fine, be an idiot. And a major jerk. I never thought you'd be a quitter. You'll regret this, mark my words."

"Mark my words? What are you, my grandmother?"

"Screw you, Logan. Walk your own sorry ass home. I'm done trying to beat some sense into your thick skull." He tossed Logan's jacket at him and it bounced off his chest onto the sidewalk. Pivoting on his heel, Sam stomped toward the parking lot.

Logan snatched up his jacket and turned away. He did *not* need this bull-crap.

Anger hastened his steps. By the time he stomped the few blocks home, his feet hurt worse than standing all day at work. He stormed inside, slamming the door behind him. A careless toss landed the jacket near the coat rack. It puddled on the floor unheeded.

An excited bark led him through the kitchen to the back foyer.

"Hey Max." He swung open the kennel door and Max popped out to sit patiently at Logan's feet. His tail swishing eagerly side by side, Max's head came above Logan's knee. Barely over a year old, Max still had a lot of puppy in him and loved to run. He was taking well to his rigid training schedule, working toward becoming a full-fledged search and rescue dog.

"Good boy," Logan praised Max's obedience. "Need to go out?"

Max responded with one soft bark.

"Okay." Opening the door, Logan let him out and watched through the window as Max hurried to the far back corner of the yard to relieve himself in his designated area. The training to get him there had been interminable and Logan had despaired of ever succeeding, but now Max never failed to hit the right spot, which kept the yard clean. Max bounced back and forth across the yard chasing the fluffy snowflakes that had begun to fall.

His eager attitude and playfulness lightened the load on Logan's heart. There was still something good in the world. After a few minutes of uninhibited play, Logan knocked twice on the door and Max hurried back to the house.

Too bad women weren't as trainable as dogs.

Chapter Seventeen

Tea rolled over and slapped her alarm clock off. Six a.m. came excessively early. She'd been awake most of the night, re-running her argument with Logan over and over in her head. She couldn't understand what drove his irritation; it was irrational. She hadn't been drinking. He didn't even try to give her the benefit of the doubt. He just acted as judge and jury, pronouncing her guilty.

"What a jerk; if I had been drunk, as my friend, you'd think he'd make sure I got home unscathed rather than coming unglued." The sound of her voice was like shards of glass ripping through her brain.

She rolled over in bed and struggled to sit on the edge of the bed, her head cupped in her hands, her elbows on her knees. She had a three-alarm hangover in spite of being stone cold sober all night. Sucking in a deep breath, she tried to get a grip on her emotions. Her nose was plugged solid, and she had a crying-jag headache.

Last night she had indulged herself with an extraordinarily selfish and atypical pity party. What the heck had she been thinking? She knew better than to risk her heart, but she'd done it anyway. Foolishly she'd let Logan in, let him get close. And heartbreak was her reward. When would she ever learn?

Well, she was finished feeling sorry for herself. It was over. Kaput. It was time to get on with her life. She took a long, hot shower, dressed and made her way downstairs, vowing to focus on the positive.

She turned on the oven, knowing that Cynthia would have prepped today's cookie dough in advance. The day felt oppressive, like she was moving through thick molasses. Coffee. She needed coffee; there was no way tea was going to cut through the sludge in her brain. The debate between espresso and regular was a short one. She'd need more than one cup and her stomach wouldn't handle too many espressos. She started coffee, thanking heaven for the industrial quick-brew pot.

The display case was virtually empty but the gleaming chrome industrial fridge held today's cookies, ready to bake. This was something her grandmother had started. All the cookies she sold were refrigerator or icebox cookies. Prepare, chill or freeze, slice and bake as needed. Cynthia had chosen two of their standards, oatmeal raisin and chocolate chip. Tea popped open the lid of the third container, to discover a triangular roll of tan and orange cookie dough that looked like candy corn. Also nestled in the container were cooking instructions and chocolate sprinkles for topping them.

Her industrial oven was huge. It easily held six trays of cookies simultaneously. She'd barely laid out the first sheets of cookies when Riley knocked on the locked front door.

"You're up early," Tea greeted her after opening the door.

"I am. Are you okay?" She studied her friend carefully.

"I'm okay. A bit fragile, maybe battered, but okay." She turned away and returned to the kitchen to pour coffee for them both. "It's going to be a ten coffee and two dozen cookies day. And I might end it with a chocolate binge." Her laugh rang hollow.

"Have you talked to him?" Her words were soft, as if she was trying not to offend.

"I have no intention of ever speaking to him again."

"Is that wise?"

"Is what wise?" Willow chorused from the doorway. She gave them a jaunty wave and clicked the deadbolt shut before joining them at the counter.

"I think Tea should talk to Logan. Maybe he has a reason for losing it last night."

"I heard about that. She probably should discuss their issues with him, but not now. Not while the wounds are still raw. She needs to find a way to forgive him." She waved away their expressions of disagreement. "Not because he deserves it, but because Tea needs it. Harboring all that anger and hurt isn't good for the soul. She needs to release it."

"I have released it," Tea snapped. "I set him free last night. We're done."

"Oh sweetie." Willow rounded the counter and pulled Tea into her embrace. "You haven't released it. You're vibrating with anger and hurt."

Tea stepped back from her friend. "Maybe. But right now, I don't even want to think about him. How could he even think that of me? How could he be so cruel? We've known each other for over half our lives, he should know better."

"Yes, he should," Riley interjected. "But, he may have a reason..."

"He's a donkey's behind." Tea slapped her hands on the counter. "Oh, butternut." The stinging in her hands almost distracted her from the hurt in her heart.

The stove beeped, indicating the preheat cycle was complete. Slipping into oven mitts, she popped the first trays in and set the timer before turning back to her friends.

"I think," Riley advised, "that you should talk to him."

"I don't," she countered and gulped down half her coffee, nearly scalding her tongue in the process.

"You should talk to him."

"Why?" Tea's voice carried her doubts.

"Chalk it up to my career. I sometimes deal with things that give me a different perspective." She shrugged, indicating that she couldn't say more.

Riley worked for Anderson & Anderson, a local law firm and was privy to a plethora of confidential information. Tea knew that her friend would never divulge client secrets, but she must believe she had an important point.

"Logan can kiss my backside. I tried, I tried hard to prove that I'm not who I used to be. He won't accept that. He's made his bed and now he can lie in it."

He could suck it up. She didn't feel forgiving at all right now. Maybe she'd feel different in a few days, or weeks, or months; but not today. Neither Willow nor Riley would let up on this unless she agreed to try to talk to him.

"I'll think about it." She held up a hand to forestall their words. "*I can't think about that right now. If I do, I'll go crazy. I'll think about that tomorrow*," she drawled in her best Scarlett O'Hara imitation, not caring that she didn't have the words quite right.

Even though Riley and Willow sniggered along with her, Tea knew they were more worried than amused.

Chapter Eighteen

The wind howled in Tea's ears as she trudged down the street toward the Thurston Hotel and a tea date with Riley. She would have preferred to meet at the shop, but Riley had insisted. There must be some final plans to check out at the hotel for Riley and Brock's wedding. Before agreeing to be Riley's maid of honor, Tea never would have guessed how much work went into planning a wedding. The details and decisions were never-ending. Of course, Riley's mother didn't help matters at all.

Lilith had her own ideas of what her daughter's wedding should entail and pushed for them, often against Riley's wishes. More than once since their engagement Tea had to step up and remind Lilith that her wishes conflicted with Riley's. The most tragically laughable disagreement had been over the wedding dress. One would think that it would be the bride's choice. Sometimes Riley gave in to her mother more than she should. Compromise could be a difficult thing.

Compromise! Ha! If only Logan understood the concept. He'd refused to listen to her the other night. He'd leaped to the conclusion that she was drinking and ignored any other explanations. She sighed heavily. Men! She was not going to focus on Logan. She wouldn't let him sour her mood. He wasn't worth it.

She stepped into the hotel, stomped the snow off her knee-high boots and wiped them clean. She slipped out of the oversized, tan wool jacket she'd adopted from her grandfather's closet when he passed away. She'd been through several ladies' jackets in the years since his death, but none of them held up like this one. It wore like iron and was warm, cozy and soft to the touch. She cast a distracted wave at Angelina at the front desk as she went by.

The Alberta Rose Coffee Shop was hopping. Most of the tables were full; the servers scurried between tables like buzzing bees. Riley waved from the back corner and Tea hurried to join her. She stuffed her fuchsia hand-knit scarf into the sleeve of her jacket and hung it over a spare chair and slid into her seat.

"Sorry, I'm late. I was distracted on the way over. I got lost in my thoughts and missed my turn. I had to walk an extra two blocks." She laughed at her comment. "Not that I don't need the exercise."

"No worries. And you don't need to work out. You're perfect."

"I've missed my run three times this week. If I don't get back on the nutrition wagon, I'll start to feel sluggish." She chuckled. "Like a bear slipping into hibernation." She glanced around the room. "Where's your mother?"

"At home, where she belongs." They shared an amused smile.

"Driving you nuts?"

"She's in full panic. And she heard about the bachelorette party." Riley groaned. "She was heading into an endless lecture when I 'accidentally' hung up on her. And I 'forgot' my cell phone at home."

"That's going to push her off the deep end," Tea advised.

"Frankly, I don't care. I need a break from her. That's why I suggested getting out."

"Well," Tea said gesturing to herself, "here I am. Time to relax."

Charity Wong, her dark hair sleek and shiny, stepped up to their table. "Ladies, can I take your order?"

"Coffee and whole wheat toast for me, please," Tea requested.

"Coffee and the breakfast special for me," Riley chuckled. "I'm starved."

"I worked up an appetite last night." She winked and Tea laughed.

"Isn't Brock away for the weekend?"

"He came home early to surprise me. Gosh, I love that man." She sighed. "I sound like a love-struck ninny."

"You do, and you should. Your wedding will be here before you know it and then off to the honeymoon. You guys are so good together. You deserve to be smitten."

For a moment, Tea envied her bestie. Love wasn't something to sneer at. It was a gift. Finding the right man and knowing you'd be happy with him was something special. Too bad not everyone was lucky enough to experience that.

"Riley, Chastity, good morning." Mrs. Arbuckle stood beside their table smiling down at them. "Mind if I join you? I've got a craving for an extra cup of coffee this morning."

Tea doubted that was true. Mrs. A. didn't do anything without a reason. If she wanted to sit with them, she must have an opinion to share.

"We'd love to have you join us," Riley responded before Tea could formulate an answer.

The town matriarch eased into the chair, smoothing her silk blouse and placing her feet primly and properly in front of her. "So, there was a bit of excitement last night."

Tea groaned.

"Stiff upper lip, Chastity. Never let them see your distress." Mrs. A. patted Tea's hand. "When I catch up to that Logan Wright, I'm going to give him a piece of my mind. What was he thinking creating a scene like that? Absolutely unacceptable."

"He was upset; don't be too hard on him."

"Chastity Howell, you aren't defending his unconscionable actions are you?" Mrs. A pinned her with a reproving glare.

"Well, he does have a history." Riley defended.

"A person cannot let the past dictate their behavior. It's high time that boy decided whether or not he's going to forgive Chastity for her mistake. It was tragic, but there comes a point when you have to suck it up and move on. Avoiding discussing your blunders or sweeping them under the carpet doesn't fix anything. It leads to hurt feelings and bigger mistakes."

"Speak of the devil..."

Mrs. A and Riley followed Tea's glance to where Logan stood in the doorway searching for someone.

"Perfect timing," Mrs. A declared and waved Logan toward them.

His brow wrinkled and his lips pressed together into a hard, thin line, but he obeyed her summons as if it came from the Queen herself. He smiled and nodded at the dowager. "Nice to see you, Mrs. Arbuckle. Riley. Chas."

Disappointment darkened Tea's heart. She'd thought he was going to stick to calling her Tea but he regressed to the hurtful nickname. How many times were they going to have this same old battle?

"Sit," Mrs. A declared.

"No thank you. I was looking for Sam Quinn. He's not here. So I'll just be going."

"Not before I'm done with you." She yanked his hand and he stumbled into the chair.

Tea refused to look at him. She searched the room, her gaze flying about, looking for a reason to escape the upcoming meddling. She'd like to get up and walk away, but she owed it to Riley to find out why they were here.

Wait! Riley hadn't set this up, had she?

Tea gave her friend a questioning look.

Riley responded with a confused shrug.

Okay, she hadn't arranged it. She was as much in the dark as Tea.

"I think," Mrs. A began, "that you and Chastity need to clear the air between you over the accident."

"I've tried, but it seems she's fallen into her old habits," he snapped, glancing at the floor.

"I have not!" Tea exploded. His words slashed into her heart and sucked the air from her chest.

"Either way," Mrs. A proclaimed, clearly not choosing sides, "you have to talk it out. That is if you ever expect to be friends again. I know you have feelings for her."

Tea could tell that her old friend was revving up for a full- blown lecture. "Let it go, Mrs. A. There is nothing between Logan and me. We were friends a long time ago, nothing more."

"Don't you try and pull the wool over my eyes, young lady. You love this man and he loves you. You're both too stubborn to admit it and try to get beyond a tragic accident."

Tea felt her mouth drop open. "Um...er..."

"I don't love her." Logan's words trampled Tea's stammering.

His denial cut deeply through her; she jerked to her feet.

"Listen, Riley, I have to run. I'll catch up with you later." She didn't bother saying goodbye to anyone else. She dropped some cash on the table, snatched up her jacket and scurried out of the café.

Chapter Nineteen

Logan stomped into The Tea Shop. He didn't want to be here. Every fiber of his being wanted to cut and run. Somebody else should be doing the shop's annual inspection. Hell, it wasn't even his turn, but Sam had insisted that Logan do it.

Considering that Sam was Logan's best friend, he sure was being an ass about this. He was trying to force the two of them together at every opportunity. They'd nearly come to blows over it. Logan winced. His knuckles hurt like the Dickens where he'd punched Sam in the gut and hit his belt buckle instead. They'd brawled for a few minutes, with both of them getting in a few good shots before Logan submitted and agreed to do the inspection. At the time it seemed like a good idea to stand up for himself, but in hindsight, it was a good thing Sam was his best friend as well as his superior or the fight might have cost him his job. Damned if women didn't cause men to go stupid.

Tea glanced up from the cash register, took one look at him and headed for the stairwell.

"Miss Howell," he called out coldly. "It's time for your inspection. I'll need your presence and your cooperation with this."

She froze in her tracks in the open doorway. He heard her exasperated breath from across the room. She closed the door, not quite slamming it and turned around. Everyone in the shop, staff and customers alike, were riveted to their conversation. Small towns were such a pain. Everyone knew their neighbor's business and nobody hesitated to snoop if it might prove interesting. She glared around the room. Some people looked away. Her friends looked back with sympathy.

"Fine. Let's get this over with. Where do you want to start?"

"The kitchen." He feigned nonchalance and greeted Willow. Keeping his questions coldly impersonal, he toured the shop checking fire extinguishers, exits and smoke detectors. He kept meticulous notes as they went. She answered his queries with equal professionality.

"I'll need to inspect your apartment because it's part of the building," he informed her. He managed to suppress a wince at her glare. He followed her up the stairs.

Damn, she might not be the woman for him, but she sure had a nice ass.

"Stop staring at my behind. You had your chance at it. So keep your eyes and your hands off." He felt a grin tug at the corners of his mouth. Chastity Howell had always been a spitfire, that's one of the things he loved about her. He slammed the brakes on that thought.

He. Did. Not. Love. Her.

Or anything about her.

***

Tea glared at Logan as he walked through her apartment. He didn't miss a single thing, not even the personal female appliance that peeked out from under the pillows on her unmade bed and made him quirk one eyebrow at her. Well, he could speculate all he wanted. Her sex life or lack of one was none of his business.

"A little advance warning might have been nice," she snapped to cover her embarrassment at having to deal with her own needs. And damn him anyway for re-stoking those needs and then abandoning her.

"The entire purpose of the inspection is to catch you off guard. I'm looking for violations."

"Well, I feel violated all right." She glared at him, wishing that the power of her stare could explode his head.

"Suck it up, princess. I'm just doing my job."

"Bite me," she snarled. "You're going out of your way to be intrusive and ignorant. Your professionality is crappy."

"Crappy? My professionality is crappy?" he snapped. "You're accusing me of being unprofessional. Get a grip, Chas. I'm not treating you any differently than any other business owner."

"You could have sent someone else." She spat the words out.

"You think I didn't try? How the hell do you think I got this black eye?"

"Words hurt?" she snapped sarcastically, crossing her arms over her chest. Dang it all, now she wanted to give him ice for the painful-looking bruises. Butternut! She was a wimp and a freaking marshmallow heart. He was a jerk and all she could think of besides her raging anger was healing his wounds.

"No, fists hurt." Disdain dripped from his words. "Sam and I had a fist fight over it."

"You hate me that much that you'd fight to stay out of here?" Tears brimmed in her eyes.

"That's not it," he sighed and flopped down on the couch. "I don't hate you, but I can't stand to look at you, knowing you're killing yourself with alcohol. But hey, what's one more death in a long chain?"

"Oh, for Pete's sake. For the very last and final time. I. Do. Not. Drink. I've been clean and sober for years. Get over it and stop being an idiot."

She raced into the bathroom and slammed the door behind her. She was not going to let him see her tears. He didn't deserve to know how badly his blind stupidity hurt her. "Go back to work, Logan. Email me your report."

He tapped on the door. "I can't do that, Chas. I have to give you a verbal report and you have to sign the paperwork before I go."

She exploded out of the bathroom. "Chas? We're back to Chas? Call me Chastity," she growled through gritted teeth. "Chastity, or better yet, Miss Howell. Give me your damned report and get out of my house." She mentally gloated when he stumbled backward from her wrath.

"You have three violations. You have three working days to correct them or I'll shut you down."

"Seriously? You're making up violations just to piss me off? You'd go to that kind of crazy length to hurt me?"

His shoulders slumped and for a brief second, she regretted her words.

"No, you failed three tests." His voice was calm and even for the first time since entering the shop. "First: the back gate sticks. It's on the property and would be used in the event of an emergency evacuation; you need a new latch. Second: the smoke detector in the upstairs kitchen has a dead battery, as does the one in the utility room downstairs. Third: the fire extinguisher by the back door expires in two days."

"So it's not actually a violation then," she demanded, glaring at him, her arms crossed angrily over her chest.

"Technically no, but it goes in the warning section. It would for anyone. Sign at the bottom." He handed her the clipboard.

She signed it and threw it at him, nicking him in the shoulder with one corner.

"You do know that it's a breach of law to assault a fire inspector?"

"Yeah well; you can breach my doorway and get out of here. And leave through the shop. I don't want anyone thinking I'm up here with you. I want nothing to do with you." She stabbed toward the stairs with one finger. "Thank you for your inspection."

"Thank you for your cooperation," he mocked. "I'll be back in three days to ensure that you've corrected your violations." He left, closing the door gently behind him.

"I'm the only one who's been violated," she whispered toward the door and let the tears fall.

Light knocking on the door alerted her to the arrival of someone else.

"Tea, are you okay?" Jade's voice came through the door.

"Come in, I'm fine."

"Willow called me," she said by way of an explanation and sat beside Tea, encompassing her in a warm hug. "If it helps, we could hear shouting, but not actual words downstairs."

"Oh great, that's exactly what I needed." She dashed away angry tears. "He did it, just like I knew he would. He took his anger out on me and failed the shop's inspection," she wailed.

"Did he?"

"Okay, not really," she pouted. "But there's stuff to fix. He could have let me pass; he could have taken my word that I'd fix it. He should have trusted me."

"And risk his job? Does he even have that in him?"

"No," she sighed and blew her nose into the tissue Jade handed her.

"Come on, honey. Everyone knows there've been issues between you for years. You had it good for a while. The whole town is rooting for you guys. People can get past their issues and mend relationships. Look at Jason and me. We managed."

"Logan can't get beyond the accident. I think it's because his mother was drinking too." She sniffed the words out, wishing she didn't understand and empathize with his issues.

"Oh, honey, substance abuse affects ninety percent of the population in some fashion. Smoking, drugs, alcohol, gambling. It hurts us all. You and I know that better than most."

Tea laughed weakly.

"And Willow says that Sam says that Logan's a wreck too. I swear by all that's holy that this will work out for you. Now, wash your face, dry those tears and get back downstairs. The last thing he needs is to hear that you're pining over him. Let him think you don't give a crap."

Chapter Twenty

A soft tinkling sound alerted Tea that someone was in the shop. She rolled over in bed and glanced at the clock. Three-thirty in the morning? Well, that ruled out the intruder being a member of her staff, unless Willow was on the midnight prowl again. When she couldn't sleep Willow holed up in her room downstairs, taking comfort in her sacred Wiccan surroundings. Maybe she forgot to shut it off. Still, she needed to ensure it wasn't a burglar.

Slipping into sweat pants and a T-shirt, she grabbed her cell phone and snuck down the stairs. As she reached the bottom, she heard a low agonized groan.

What the heck? Someone was hurt. She pressed 911 on her phone but didn't hit send. Instead she eased back the deadbolt and cracked the door open.

Diffuse illumination from the streetlights filtered through the blinds; but the room was virtually dark. She needed internal security lights. She could barely see anything. What was that? Something moved near the counter.

Someone was writhing in agony on the floor sobbing softly.

Whoever it was must be hurt.

She slipped the phone back into her pocket Tea stepped through the doorway.

"Help me," the girl cried.

Tea hurried across the room and knelt down. "Are you okay?"

"No," she wailed. "I think I'm in labor."

"Destiny?"

She curled up in a ball and screamed.

"Breathe, honey. Slow deep breaths. I'll get you some help."

Destiny's hand shot out and grabbed Tea's arm. "Don't go. Help me."

"Okay, honey. Breathe. The contraction will pass in a minute." She hoped like hell that she was telling the truth. After a few interminable seconds, Destiny relaxed.

"What are you doing out in this weather? You should be at home."

"I don't have a home. I had a bellyache. My back hurts. I can't take drugs," she panted. "I went for a walk. Sometimes that helps."

"Not this time," Tea chuckled. "This time I think you're going to need a doctor. Let's get you out of this jacket." She filed away the fact that Destiny didn't have a home for further consideration. She couldn't think about it now; there was too much going on.

Destiny groaned in agony as they worked together to get her out of her coat. Tea helped her into a semi-sitting position, making her squeal in distress.

"Oh my god, oh my god, oh my god."

"What?" Tea demanded. "What is it?"

Tears streaked down Destiny's face. "I think my water broke. Everything's wet." She sobbed incoherently. "You were so nice to me and I've wrecked your shop."

Tea chuckled. "Oh sweetheart, it's tile. It'll clean. A mop and some bleach and it'll be as good as new."

"I'm so sorry," Destiny wailed as another contraction overcame her.

How long was that? Three minutes? Less? They needed help. Fast.

"I'm going to call an ambulance."

"I can't pay–" a groan cut off her words.

"Let me worry about that." She dialed the firehall.

A familiar voice answered.

"Logan. Thank god," Tea exclaimed. "I've got a pregnant girl in labor in the shop, on the floor. Get over here fast."

Destiny clutched her arm. The phone clattered away. In the distance, Tea heard Logan's voice calling out to her.

"Get over here, now!" she shouted at the phone.

Thirty seconds later, someone was pounding on the back door.

"I have to get this," she told Destiny. "Hang tough. It's the ambulance."

She sprinted down the hallway and opened the door. Logan exploded through, dressed in jeans and his ever-present fire department T-shirt.

"Are you okay?" he demanded.

"I'm fine. It's Destiny. Remember her, the pregnant girl? She's in labor." Destiny screamed, cutting off Tea's words. They bolted down the hall.

Tea skidded to a stop and kneeled beside the distraught teenager. "It's okay. Help is here. This is my friend, Logan. He's a fireman. He's going help us through this." She stroked Destiny's hair off her face and held her hand.

"Hi," Logan said. "I'm here to help, but I'm going to have to examine you. What's your name, sweetheart?"

"Destiny," she moaned.

"Okay, Destiny. Tea and I are going to help you out of your pants, so I can check you over."

"No!" She tried to scramble to her feet.

"It's okay." Tea comforted her. "You can trust him. I trust him with my life." As the words came out, she realized that she meant it.

"No, he's...he's..."

"He's what?" Tea asked, straining for patience.

"He's too hot," the girl groaned.

Logan grinned and Tea chuckled.

"He is at that," she agreed. "But we can't worry about that now. I promise you he'll be nothing but professional. Even when he's a pain in my rear end, he's all pro."

Logan snorted.

"I'll close my eyes until the last second," he promised. Sirens started in the distance.

"'kay," Destiny agreed reluctantly.

Tea draped her with a towel and helped her out of her pants and onto a pile of towels she'd grabbed from the kitchen. Logan assisted as best he could with his eyes closed.

"Okay, Destiny, I have to look now. It's me or one of the other six guys that'll be here any second. Spread your legs a bit and let me see."

"God, this is so humiliating," Destiny groaned and squeezed her eyes shut. "I'm sorry about the mess," she moaned as she opened her legs.

Logan did a quick exam, explaining his actions as he went. Chastity watched his every move and stroked Destiny's head and arms, murmuring comforting words.

"Okay, Destiny. We don't have time to get to the hospital. You're going to have to do this here."

"On the floor," she squeaked.

"On a blanket," he corrected. "Toss me a blanket, Sam."

Tea looked up to see Sam and the rest of their crew hovering in the hallway.

"Oh my god," Destiny cried. "Get them out of here. I don't want them staring at my..."

"Back away, guys. Sam, hand me that blanket. Destiny, look at me."

She glared up at Logan.

"Destiny, I can't do this alone. Sam is going to have to help us. This is my partner and best friend, Sam."

"Oh god, he's cute too."

Chastity laughed. "Girl, this town doesn't have an ugly fireman; and you're in the best hands right now. Logan and Sam are the best medics in town." She flashed an apologetic grin at the rest of the group and they smiled in understanding.

With a bit of effort, they managed to get her onto a blanket before the baby arrived. Several long and agonizing minutes later, an irate baby came into the world squalling and screaming.

Tears poured down Destiny's face. "Don't tell me what it is. Just take it away. I can't keep him."

Logan gave Tea a questioning glance.

She shrugged her confusion.

"What is it, honey?"

"I can't keep him. I love him already and I can't keep him. I have to give him up. If I see him I won't be able to," she wailed. "He needs more than I can give him."

Tea wrapped her in an embrace. "It will be okay, Logan will look after the baby. I'll meet you at the hospital and we'll figure out what to do. You don't have to look at your baby."

Briskly efficient, they bundled her onto a stretcher and out into the ambulance. Logan followed with the wrapped baby, careful to keep the infant out of Destiny's vision. With the teenager settled, Tea went to step out.

"No!" Destiny squealed. "Stay with me. I need you."

"It's okay, Tea. You can come," Logan advised. "We don't usually let non-family ride along, but this time we'll make an exception."

Doctor Sheridan met them at the emergency entrance. Destiny was hustled away to one room with Chastity. Logan accompanied the baby to another.

During the examination, Destiny told her story.

"My parents kicked me out when they found out I was pregnant," she said with resigned acceptance. "They didn't even care that I was raped. They wouldn't help me. God was punishing me for my sins," she snapped. "That's what they said." Tears trickled down her face.

Tea patted her hand comfortingly.

"I wanted an abortion. I couldn't keep a job because I was so sick. It took forever to save enough money and when I found a place to do it, they said I was too far along. I didn't know what to do." She wailed in full meltdown mode. "I stowed away on a bus and ended up here. Bonnie Reid let me stay in the shed behind Melanie Larson's house. We fixed it up nice. She snuck me food. She's been my best friend. Everyone here is so kind. You fed me." She gave Tea a wobbly smile that almost broke Tea's heart.

"Now, I have a baby I can't look after. I don't know what to do." She sobbed uncontrollably.

Tea's mind skittered around, trying to find a way to support her and finally lit on an idea.

"I'll call my friend. Riley works in a law office; she'll know what to do. We'll find that baby a good home. Then, when you get out of this hospital, we'll help you get back on your feet. I'll let Bonnie know you're okay."

"Thank you," Destiny wailed. "I don't deserve this."

"Honey, this isn't your fault. Someone attacked you. Your family acted like jerks. We'll get you through this. How old are you?"

"Seven...seven...seventeen," she stammered.

"Not an adult yet; that might be an issue, but Riley'll know who to talk to."

Eventually, Destiny calmed down enough to sleep. Tea wanted nothing more than to go home and rest herself, but things had to be set in motion. She scratched out a note for Destiny, telling her she'd be back soon and leaving her phone number.

She bumped into Dr. Sheridan in the hallway. "She's sleeping. I'm going to go home and catch a nap."

"Legally, I can't talk to you about this," the doctor informed her. "But you came in with her and she insisted that you be here for everything. So I'm calling you her legal guardian, for the time being."

Tea nodded.

"She's fine. A little undernourished, and overtired, but fine overall. The delivery didn't cause any undue damage." He smiled and Tea relaxed. "The baby, a boy, is healthy too. As per her wishes, we'll keep them separate and won't talk about him, unless she changes her mind. She'll need to talk to a child advocate, for them. That needs to happen quickly. We can set that up if you like."

"I called Riley. She'll set something up in the morning."

"Good enough then. You go get some sleep; you look wiped. Do you need Cynthia to work tomorrow? She's on another of those infernal professional days from school."

"That would be good. Thank you. For everything. I'm off to bed."

She turned and headed for the exit. She debated taking a taxi home, but didn't have her purse with her. She'd have to walk.

***

Logan leaned against the wall, waiting. He didn't feel a bit guilty about eavesdropping outside Destiny's room or listening to Tea's conversation with the doctor. Try as he might, he couldn't discount how impressed he was at her attitude through this whole debacle. Troublesome teens and emergency deliveries were nothing new for him, but he was relatively sure they were outside her wheelhouse. She'd captivated him with her natural calm.

"Need a ride?" he asked. She jerked her head toward him. He'd startled her.

"Oh gosh, yes. Thanks, Logan. I'm beyond tired." Her voice quivered with exhaustion.

"You were amazing, kept calm and rational through the whole thing. I knew you were strong, but I didn't know you had that in you." His praise echoed his earlier thoughts.

"How did you beat the ambulance to the shop?" She suddenly realized that he'd beaten it by several minutes.

"It's a short run, barely half a block. The rest of the guys had to suit up. I sprinted down the alley. You needed me, I came." The words shocked him, and judging by the look on her face, they startled her too.

"Wait, you came with us in the ambulance. How'd your truck get here?" she asked climbing in.

He chuckled. "I had the guys bring it over while I waited for you. They locked up the shop too." He dug in his pocket, pulled out her keys and tossed them into her lap.

"Oh, thanks."

"Don't sound so surprised. If you need me, I'll be there for you, no matter what our relationship is, or isn't. I might not be the man for you, but I'm not an asshole," he grumbled and started the truck.

"No, you aren't. You're a good man, Logan Wright." She leaned over and kissed him on the cheek. "You're a good man."

Her praise touched him. She was such an enigma, so strong-willed and so kind all at once. If he lived to be hundred and six, he'd never unravel the mystery that was Chastity Howell.

She leaned back against her seat and was asleep before he got out of the hospital parking lot. He drove slowly, stealing glances at her as he went. He took the long way home, turning a three-block ride into something closer to thirty blocks, allowing him to watch her sleep. It was a dangerous game for his peace of mind. He drove slowly and cautiously along the empty streets.

Even in her exhaustion, she was beautiful. The realization hit him that he still loved her. He didn't want to, and he wished he didn't, but there was no denying it. He might always love her, in spite of, or maybe because of, everything that happened between them. He just didn't know what to do about it.

Chapter Twenty-One

"Hey, Logan," Sam called down the fire station hallway.

Logan stuck his head out of the station kitchen doorway. "What's up?"

"I need you to make a run over to the hotel. Mrs. Arbuckle is worried about a fire safety violation."

"Can't someone else go?" he complained. "I'm halfway through making lasagna for supper. You know how she is; I'll be there for hours. Send the new guy." He wiped his hands on a towel.

Sam laughed. "She's a doll and yes, you'll be there for a while, but she asked specifically for you. She said, and I quote, 'Send that adorable Mr. Wright.'" He chuckled. "I'll finish cooking."

"And eat it too, no doubt. You know there isn't going to be a violation. The Thurston Hotel always passes their safety inspections with flying colors. The old girl's up to something and I'm not sure I want to find out what."

"Go, shoo." Sam chuckled and flicked his hands toward the door. "And take the station pickup, just in case there is something amiss; we don't want to look sloppy."

Logan groaned.

Ten minutes later, he tapped on the door of Mrs. Arbuckle's suite, notebook and pen in hand.

The door popped open in a flash. Mrs. A smiled up at him and smoothed her snow-white hair. "Why Logan, do come in." She gestured grandly for him to enter the suite.

Inside the room, a rolling trolley from the kitchen was set up in front of the small settee. It held a pot of tea, some cookies and two generous slices of chocolate cake. Mrs. A was definitely up to something.

"Sit down and let's chat."

He perched on the edge of a chair and flipped open his notebook. "I understand that you believe the hotel has some potential fire safety violations?" he queried.

"Oh my," she chuckled. "That might have been a wee bit of an exaggeration. Tea?"

"What about her?"

Mrs. A smirked and gave a tinkling giggle. "No, no. I meant would you like a cup of tea. Why ever would you think I meant Miss Howell?"

"Well," he hesitated. "She does like to be called Tea, and we recently dated. But, no thank you. I'll pass on a beverage." Good gravy, he had to stop thinking about Chastity, and a relationship that would never be.

"Don't be silly." She poured them both tea and handed him a cup. He dropped the notepad rather than let the tea she thrust at him hit the floor.

"Are there any violations?" he asked, striving for patience. What was it about the old people in Harmony that made them think they had the right to meddle in his business?

"No, dear. There aren't any violations. Mr. A and I thought we should discuss this whole nasty Chastity business with you and clear up a few points."

"Mr. A?" he questioned. "Ma'am, your husband is dead," he said kindly.

"Of course he is," she replied as if Logan were stupid. "That doesn't mean I don't talk to him on occasion. He's quite good at keeping me company, though some days I'm worried that his being here keeps him from moving on to a better place." She smiled sadly. Her smile morphed into a grin. "Enough about my Walter, let's talk about you."

"I really should be getting back to the station."

"Nonsense, that nice Samuel Quinn assured me that you had all the time you need. He said he'd call your cell phone if they required anything of you."

Logan sighed and leaned back in the chair, bracing himself for a long uncomfortable discussion. "Let's get this over with," he said and picked up his cup. When he got back to the station, he was going to beat Sam senseless for getting him into this.

"How is your father? Is he enjoying Texas?" She sipped at her tea regally, pinkie finger extended.

"He's doing well. He golfs a lot with my uncle. They'll both be back when my sister gets married. And he'll come home for Christmas." Logan banked down a sigh. This would last an eternity if she kept beating around the bush like this.

"And do you talk often?"

"A couple times a week. We keep updated on Facebook too. He sends the twins and me pictures of his golfing and their travels as well."

"I've thought about getting The Facebook. But not too many of my friends are as technologically savvy as I am. It would probably be a waste of time."

Logan chuckled. Mrs. A tech-savvy? Not in this lifetime. "Well, if you ever want to set up an account I could help you out."

"An account? Is it expensive?"

"It's free. But you'd need a computer."

"Nonsense. I don't need a computer. I'll just use the telephone like regular people."

Logan set his half-empty cup down, hoping to escape.

"Oh, are you ready for your cake?" She thrust a plate at him. The slice of chocolate cake was enormous; the weight of it nearly toppled the plate out of his hand.

"Um. Thanks. This is huge. Would you like some of it?"

"What I would like…is to know what's going on in that crazy head of yours. I thought you and Chastity had finally worked out your differences."

"Mrs. A, no offense, but I really don't want to discuss my love life with you." He sighed. If only she was that easy to shut down.

"So it is love then?"

"What Chastity and I had, whatever it was, is over." His plate clattered onto the trolley and he stood to go.

"Sit. This conversation isn't over yet, young man. Show some respect." She waggled her finger at him and then nibbled demurely on a cookie.

He closed his eyes, searching for calm. He might as well get this over with; if he left now, she'd keep calling the station and drive the entire fire department insane with her incessant demands.

He picked up his cake and took a small bite. It was probably delicious, the food at The Thurston always was. It could have been cardboard for all he noticed. Nothing tasted right these days.

"So, tell me about this baby you delivered. And on the floor of The Tea Shop, no less."

Logan grinned. "That was something. Tea called the station in a panic because someone was in labor in her shop. I raced over, the rest of the crew followed. Destiny, that's the mom's name, had the baby right there on the floor. Tea was magnificent. She didn't panic. She kept calm and helped Destiny get through it."

"That's my Chastity, she's a strong one that girl."

"She is. But her strength surprised me."

"She was sober then?"

Logan paused, mid-bite. She had been sober; he just hadn't considered it before now.

"She was sober. At least I didn't smell anything on her breath," he said, qualifying the statement. "And she wasn't shaking or showing any signs of a hangover."

"Excellent." Mrs. A clapped her hands excitedly. "I was hoping she was still sober. Fighting an addiction is difficult."

Logan doubted that the prim and proper Mrs. Arbuckle knew anything about addictions, but one never knew what skeletons where hiding in someone's closet. "I doubt that you've fought an addiction." He grinned at her.

"Of course not!" She feigned shock. "But I do know a lot of people and that AA group meets downstairs virtually every day. You should stop in sometime and see what they're all about."

"I don't think so, thank you."

"Are you worried about embarrassing Chastity or the other members? You needn't be. They all have to make amends to get on with their life. It's part of the twelve step program."

"I'm familiar with the twelve step program."

"Oh right, I'd forgotten about your mother."

"Life goes on," Logan parroted with a shrug. "Some things change, some things don't."

"Chastity has changed," Mrs. A advised him. "It sounds like she was wonderful with that young girl and her baby."

There was a sly tone to her voice that set Logan's teeth on edge.

"She was phenomenal. She showed real courage, they both did." It didn't hurt too badly to admit that she'd breezed through the delivery. Besides, it didn't matter because he was done with Tea. A relationship with her was just too risky.

"It sounds like she showed fabulous maternal instincts. And she's spent the last two days at the hospital helping Destiny deal with the fallout of her delivery." She took a small sip of her tea and set the cup down. She folded her hands in her lap in a take-that gesture.

"I'm glad Chastity is able to assist her. That girl's had a hard time."

"She's taken her under her wing, as if Destiny was her own child. Chastity Howell has a lot of love to give and you'll be a dang fool if you pass up the opportunity to patch up your relationship with her."

He closed his eyes and prayed for patience. This was getting old. Everyone in town was on his case for not giving Tea the benefit of the doubt. Nobody understood his perspective. Alcoholics didn't make good parents. He'd seen it with his own eyes. He'd lived it.

"I appreciate your candor, Mrs. A; but Tea and I weren't meant to be. Let it go. Please." He rose to his feet and picked up his clipboard.

The teacart lurched forward, banging him in the shins. Pain radiated up his leg making him wince. It hurt like the Dickens. He cast a wary glance at Mrs. A.

"Don't blame me," she said. She glanced across the room and said, "Walter, you stop that right now. The boy's a hard-headed fool, but he'll come to his senses." She looked at Logan apologetically. "Sorry about that. Walter's a tough one when it comes to affairs of the heart."

"You're telling me that your dead husband rammed me with a teacart?" The old girl was off her rocker if she believed that.

"You don't think I did it?" she asked, belligerence and innocence coloring her voice.

Innocent my left eye. A dead man was not punishing him for disagreeing with his wife; the thought was preposterous.

"Of course not. You wouldn't do something like that," he said dryly. "Now, if there are no fire violations, I'll head back to the station."

"Thank you for coming." She smiled broadly. "Think about what I said. Tea's a good girl and she deserves a fine upstanding man like you."

"I'll do that. Thank you for the tea and cake." He let himself out the door.

Leaning against the wall across from the elevator, he considered what she'd said. Tea did show good maternal instincts. She was strong when she needed to be with Destiny. Strong and soft, like velvet-covered steel.

However, one good moment didn't disprove a lifetime of disastrous decisions.

Chapter Twenty-Two

The clickity-clack of high heels and the muffled sound of female whispers interrupted Tea's soak in the tub.

"Chastity," Destiny's voice called apologetically through the door. "There are some ladies here to see you."

The door opened and Willow, Jade and Riley squeezed into the bathroom. Thankfully, she was chin deep in bubbles. She didn't move.

"Seriously guys, I can't have a bath without interruption?" she asked dryly.

"Nope. Get out of the tub." Jade stuck her hand in the water and pulled out the plug. "We're having an intervention."

Riley tossed a towel onto Tea's head and the trio traipsed out of the bathroom; Destiny apologized and shut the door.

"So much for a nice relaxing bath," Tea grumbled as she dried off. For a brief moment, she'd debated ignoring her friends but they'd never leave until they'd said their piece.

She slipped into flannel pajamas and joined them in the living room. Destiny apologized again. Tea kissed her on top of the head. "One thing you'll have to learn if you live here is that these three hags get their way, no matter what." She gestured to her friends and rolled her eyes.

"Hags?" Willow squawked.

"Hags!" Tea affirmed and flopped into the armchair. "I don't need an intervention," she told them. "I'm not drinking. Not that I don't want to…"

"Then why is there a bottle of whiskey by the sink?" Jade demanded.

"Oh, that."

"Yes, that," Jade echoed. "It's okay to slip."

"I didn't slip." Tea defended herself. "I came close. Too close. I bought it, I poured it, I smelled it…and I put it down and went for a bath instead." A thought hit her. "Wait, how'd you know about the whiskey?" She scrutinized each of them in turn, her stare finally landing on Destiny.

"You called them?" she asked weakly.

Destiny blushed. "I didn't know you didn't drink it. And you told me about being an alcoholic and I couldn't find the number for your sponsor." She stared down at the floor. "And I wanted to help you, like you helped me."

Her downcast, shame-faced expression broke Tea's heart. She leapt to her feet and embraced her new roommate. "Oh honey, you did the right thing. Next time, ask me first. I came close to falling off the wagon, but at the last moment, I pulled myself back on."

"Are you sure it's okay?" Destiny hesitated. "You aren't mad at me?"

"For caring about me? Heck no." She turned her expression fierce. "But I might have to tickle you to death for calling in these hags." She tickled Destiny's knees until the girl relaxed and giggled.

"You don't have to worry about things like that here, you're safe with me. Reg Anderson is working on getting me temporary guardianship of you, if your parents don't object. And he'll work with a social worker and private adoption agency to find a great family for your baby."

"My parents won't care," she said sadly.

"Harsh," Willow sympathized.

"They're...different." Destiny was defending her fanatically religious and hypercritical parents, even though they'd thrown her out after she was raped.

"Girl, your heart is too big and too soft," Willow praised. "But you'll be okay with us. Now." She rubbed her hands together, "who's up for pizza?"

"So is this a party now?" Tea joked.

"Yes and no," Riley said. "We'll celebrate your sobriety, but we need to talk about Logan."

"What's to talk about? He doesn't trust me to stay clean, and frankly, he's right to doubt me. I'm not wife or parent material. I'm a broken-down party girl with a trunk-load of issues."

"No," Jade corrected, "you're a human being who made a huge mistake. The past is the past. It shapes your future, but it's pliable clay. Nothing's set in concrete and if Logan had the stones, he'd be your champion, your rock, not the boulder that flattens you." She paused and gestured dramatically toward the desk. "Shoot, hand me something to write with, I feel a song coming on."

Tea laughed and handed over a pen and paper. "You know what they say, you can take the singer out of California but you can't take the songwriter out of the girl."

"What would you do if Logan showed up right now, and apologized?" Willow asked.

"Demand an explanation of his crappy attitude and it had better be a good one." Her eyes widened. "Oh butternut! Tell me you didn't call him," she gasped.

"No!" Destiny said. "I only called Willow."

"I called these two. Nobody called Logan." Willow gestured to the others. "But seriously, what would you do, Tea?"

A tiny glimmer, a blossom of hope unfurled in Tea's heart as she considered the question. "I'd listen to what he had to say and if it didn't measure up, I'd kick him in the nards," Tea said at last.

"And if it did?" Riley prodded.

"I'd have to think about whether or not he was worth taking another chance on." Deep inside, that tiny blossom withered, but didn't fade away completely.

Chapter Twenty-Three

Logan glanced at the old man on a bench in the park. Snowflakes covered his toque and a layer of ice hung off his beard and mustache. He really needed to be inside where it was warm so he wasn't at risk of freezing to death. In spite of his exhaustion and burning desire to be at home in bed, he stopped and checked on Mr. Zed. Tea was always concerned about her elderly friend, so Logan started a conversation in hopes of convincing him to head indoors for the night.

"Hey, Mr. Zed, how are you doing?"

"Good enough," he replied gruffly.

"Report any fires lately?"

The old man snorted. "Danged mayor gave me a civic duty medal for saving Chastity's life. Foolishness. Anybody would have done the same."

"Perhaps, but you did it, and I for one, am pleased."

"Thanks." He cleared his throat. "I saved your gal for you."

"You did, even if she isn't 'my gal.'"

"Logan Wright, for a smart man, you're pretty damned stupid." Mr. Zed shook his head sadly.

"You're a fine one to talk," Logan retorted, avoiding the inference that he was foolish to break up with Tea. "I'm not the one sleeping outside in weather cold enough to freeze grain alcohol."

Mr. Zed chortled. "I'll give you that one. But you're not getting off that easy. You'd have to be an idiot to let a fine young thing, like Chastity Howell, get away."

"Tea and I have our differences."

"You mean she's smart and you're dumber than the hind end of a mule, and about as stubborn too? I've been around this town for a long time. Hell, I've been in Harmony for twice as long as you've been on this earth. I've never seen a more suitable or stubborn couple. Hell, I've met three star generals who were less stubborn and fractious."

"I'm not that stubborn," Logan denied hotly.

"Then why are you being an ass about this?"

"You're really nosy and bossy for someone who barely knows me."

"I don't know you well, but I've watched you grow up from a boy to a young whipper-snapper and then to a man. I knew your dad, and your grandfather. And I know what happened to your mother." He paused, letting that sink in and then continued. "You're letting her death cloud your relationship with Tea. She's changed and doesn't deserve to be judged for her past sins or for your mother's sins."

"You don't know anything about my mother." What was it about Harmony that made everyone think they could stick their noses in their neighbor's business?

"I know that Tea regrets what happened."

His words surprised Logan. It was as if Mr. Zed could read Logan's mind. "You talk to her a lot?"

"Not often, but she feeds me sometimes and lets me sleep in her shed." He shrugged as if he didn't want to explain the complexity of his relationship with Tea.

"Don't you have a place to live? There are agencies…"

"I don't need no damn agency getting into my business. I have a bachelor suite in Arbuckle Arms. It's too damn claustrophobic, so I sleep outside. Besides, if I slept at home, Tea could have slept through the shop fire. Boy, you owe Destiny and me a huge debt for saving the love of your life."

The lucidity of Mr. Zed's argument surprised Logan. He'd only stopped to talk to the old guy because Tea had a soft spot for him. Until tonight, he'd concluded that Mr. Zed was off kilter…okay, he'd thought the old man was crazy, in spite of Tea's protestations to the contrary. Now, it didn't seem that way.

"I do owe you for reporting that fire. Her smoke detectors failed. She might have lost everything if not for you."

"And you'd have lost her. Can you live without her?"

The idea that Tea might have died wasn't a new one; but hearing it from someone else was like a sucker punch to the balls. It was debilitating, frightening and gut wrenchingly painful. Jesus. Could he live without her?

"I don't think I could," he whispered the words aloud, answering the question for both of them.

"I knew it," Mr. Zed crowed. "Go after her. Figure out how to deal with your problems and your fears before she gets away."

"It's not that easy." He rubbed his gloved hands down his thighs, easing the tension gathered there.

"It should be. Don't pass up love; it might never come around again. It didn't for me. I left my girl behind to join the army; she was married by the time I got back. I never found anyone like my Fancy and I still miss her. So think on it, son. Don't let her get away." He patted Logan on the shoulder.

Was it that easy? Could they just talk and work things out? The odds against making it work with Tea were astronomical.

"I'll talk to her."

"Good."

"I'll talk to her on one condition," Logan amended.

"What's that?"

"That you talk to someone about your fears. I'm guessing PTSD. There are agencies that help with that. Wouldn't you prefer to live a normal life rather than living on the streets? Wouldn't you like to have friends?"

"Tea's my friend. So is Destiny."

"Is that enough?"

"People don't make friends with crazy old men," Mr. Zed objected sadly.

"You're not crazy. I think you have your issues, but I don't think you're nuts."

"You did."

"I did," Logan admitted with a wry grin. "But Tea taught me different. She's your champion and says you're claustrophobic from being a POW. So if you get help, I'll try and work it out with her."

"I wouldn't even know where to start. There's no veterans' services in Harmony and I ain't moving."

"I'll make some calls and set something up for you. I'll find you when I have details."

"Promise you'll work it out with Tea?" he countered.

"I promise to try *if* you promise to see someone."

"Fine." He sighed dejectedly. "But it ain't gonna do no good. My head's messed up bad."

"We'll both try. Deal?" He offered his hand and they shook on the deal.

"Leave me a note in Tea's shed if you can't find me. That girl's a doll; she left me a minus thirty-degree sleeping bag. She's got the biggest heart I've ever met."

"She does. But I worry about the drinking." Dismay colored his words and spiked up his spine.

"She's lost a lot of people. Her folks, her sister, her grandparents, and your mother."

"And her best friend in high school," Logan added. "Corrie and Tea were real close."

"That's a lot of loss for one small girl."

"She's not a girl anymore, she's an adult."

"She's more than an adult; that Tea's all woman." He chuckled and winked lewdly at Logan.

"Don't you be chasing my girl," Logan warned with a laugh and stood up to continue the short walk home from the fire station. "Well, I've got to let the dog out and get some sleep. If you need anything, stop by the station and ask for me."

"I'll do that. You get on to apologizing to Tea. She needs a good man."

"Tea is strong, and independent. She doesn't need a man."

"She does and you need a good woman. So move your ass before it's too late. Good night, Logan."

"Good night, Mr. Zed. Get yourself out of the cold."

The old man stood and ambled in the general direction of The Tea Shop. Sleeping in a shed in a cold weather rated sleeping bag was better than spending the night unsheltered.

Logan watched him go. Tea had gone out of her way to provide comfort to a befuddled old man who meant nothing to her. It implied that she did have caring, maternal instincts. He wasn't sure he could reconcile that with his biases against her.

Could he be wrong?

Logan picked up his pace and hurried home. It was blistering cold out. All he wanted was a hot drink and a long sleep. Preferably without dreams of the one woman who turned his world upside down every time she entered his head.

Chapter Twenty-Four

Max sat patiently on the mat, allowing Logan to wipe the matted snow from between his toes and out of his fur.

"Come on, boy, let's have a rest." He picked up his hot chocolate and carried it into the living room. He settled down beside the fire, Max snuggled up against him, his chin on Logan's knee.

"She gave Mr. Zed a sleeping bag. Minus thirty rated sleeping bags aren't cheap, you know. Those things'll set you back a couple hundred bucks."

The dog nodded.

"Why would she do that?"

Max looked up at him with pleading soulful eyes.

"Are you on her side too?"

Max barked softly. Logan glared at the dog. Even his own damned dog had turned against him.

"She is nice, I'll give you that," he advised the dog who wagged his tail. "And cute. She's a bit like her grandmother," Logan said, stroking Max's head. "She'd do anything for anyone. She's kind to strangers. She's even taken in Destiny. Sam said she's giving the girl a home and job to get her back on her feet."

Max's tail doubled its motion, waving back and forth and banging excitedly against the floor. He looked at up Logan with sad puppy eyes.

"Come on, you don't miss her."

Max growled and walked away; he sat in the doorway with his back to Logan.

"You want me to take her back?" he asked incredulously. Max's tail thumped once. "You think she's worth the risk?" Another tail thump. "I don't know, she's an alcoholic. I've lived that one, it's heartbreaking." Max growled.

"Do you think they could be different? Everyone says they are." Max glanced at him over his shoulder and turned away again.

"Could I handle it if she lost her way and fell off the wagon? Dad didn't handle it well with Mom, and I failed there too." Regrets swamped him.

What if he'd been more understanding? What if he'd gone to meetings? Could they have banded together to pull his mother back from the precipice? Or was she too far gone? If he had done more, the accident might never have happened.

Guilt hit him between the eyes. He hadn't saved his mother, and he hadn't done enough to save Tea either.

"What ifs and should haves were useless. There's no way to see what might have been. I need to muddle this through. Okay, Max. She's been dry for years. She hasn't slipped up once, but she might. What happens then? Okay, then I'll support her. How do I do that? Meetings, it always comes back to the meetings. I guess I'll need to know what I'm up against. What about kids? Mom was good most of the time, but Dad worked away too much and left her alone."

His thoughts whirled round and round, crashing into each other like bumper cars. He was torn and conflicted. He wanted to walk away, to leave town and forget Chastity Howell ever existed.

"As if that would ever happen." He patted the floor beside him; Max glanced over and looked away. "Snubbed by my own dog," he sighed. "What if I said I want to take a chance, what if I tried again?"

Max leaped up and trotted over to Logan. His tongue flashed out and he slobbered enthusiastically all over Logan's face and hands. Logan laughed and they rolled around the floor wrestling.

"Come on, boy, let's get some sleep. I need a fresh head. I have some serious planning to do. And I'm going to need a shrink because I'm taking dating advice from a dog." He chuckled as they headed for the bedroom.

Chapter Twenty-Five

Tuesday morning dawned bright and sunny. The shop was hopping. Everyone in town was excited to see clear blue skies, even if it meant the temperatures would plummet without cloud cover to trap in heat. All the tables were full and customers lined up out the door. The bell jangled as people came and went.

Tea hurried back and forth between the register and the oven, serving customers and making more cookies. She loved the continual buzz of happy chatter that echoed through the shop. It was the sound of success and contentment. Life was perfect except for that one little hole in her heart where Logan used to be.

She chatted easily with Roger Nallos as she prepared his frou-frou coffee. They bantered back and forth with his partner on whether or not a real man drank fancy coffees. She laughed aloud at his response that men drank black coffee, not that girly crap. Her laugh echoed through the suddenly silent room.

She glanced around Roger to see what instigated the abrupt silence.

Like a dream come true, or maybe a nightmare, Logan stood at the back of the line. All eyes fixed upon him and his dog.

His dog? He couldn't have a dog in here. Her customers would be appalled–she was.

"Logan Wright, get that dog out of my shop," she called out.

"Sorry Tea, he has every right to be here."

"There's a bylaw against animals in an eating establishment."

"He's exempt," Logan claimed, grinning as he led the dog forward.

People chuckled as he came forward.

"How, pray tell, is he exempt?" She glared at him, her hands on her hips. Her heart stuttered, why was he grinning? He was up to something.

"He's a service dog?" He sauntered forward a couple more steps.

"He's a search and rescue dog, and not even a fully trained one," she countered. Strangely, she was enjoying this bantering; it felt like old times.

She peeked over the counter. Max carried a bouquet of flowers in his mouth and wore a vest stating 'service dog in training.'

"In training for what?" she blurted.

"Floral delivery?"

"That doesn't make him a service dog." She denied his attempt at a joke.

"I don't know," Roger spoke up. "He's got the vest; as an officer of the law, I have to allow it. Besides, he's got the delivery to prove it."

Tea stared slack-jawed at Roger who shrugged and stepped aside. She looked down at Max, he was grinning around the enormous bundle of daisies and carnations.

"I've come to apologize," Logan blurted.

A collective sigh rustled around the room before everyone fell silent again.

"So apologize," she demanded. There was no way she was going to give him a break, even if it was sweet that he'd pulled strings to get Max into the shop.

"Here? In front of half the town?" His gaze darted around the room.

"Here," she echoed.

He looked down, his cheeks flushed bright red and he looked at her pleadingly. She graced him with a half-smile.

His sigh of surrender was nearly her undoing. For a moment, she was tempted to let him say his piece in private.

"Chastity, I've been a jerk. I've hurt you. I've punished you repeatedly for your past sins. I couldn't see that you've changed. I refused to believe it, and for that I'm sorry."

Tears brimmed in her eyes. The urge to go to him, to embrace him was overwhelming. She clenched her fists, her nails digging into her palms and she held her ground. Waiting.

"I couldn't take a chance on you because of my past, so I cut and run to keep myself out of harm's way. It didn't work. I was hurt anyway. Mortally wounded. My heart was broken and I did it to myself."

"You did," she agreed softly. She didn't look away from him; if she made eye contact with anyone else, she'd give in. She'd be hurt again. "Tell me about your past," she suggested and almost winced at how much like an order those five words sounded.

"Here?" He pleaded. "Can we talk in private?"

"We could." She rounded the counter and accepted the flowers Max still held in his mouth. He panted his gratitude.

"But we won't," she said, turning back to look at Logan.

His eyes shimmered, his shoulders were tense, his hands fisted at his sides. His face still bore evidence of his earlier discomfort. She realized that this wasn't any easier on him than it was on her. It might even be harder for him.

"You want me to bare my soul, here?"

She nodded, unable to speak past the lump in her throat.

"You know my mom was an alcoholic, what you might not know is that I didn't do enough to stop it," he blurted.

"Oh," she gasped, her hands flew up to cover her mouth.

"She tried over and over again to get sober. It didn't work. The smallest thing would set her off on another binge." His voice was flat, unemotional, and toneless, as if he was barely controlling his feelings.

"I'm sorry," she whispered, taking a small step toward him.

"Thanks." He shrugged. "Dad was gone a lot, I don't blame him, he had to work, but I don't think that helped. I, we, James, Julia and I, never cut Mom a break. We were typical teenagers, ganging together and being jerks. We were testing our limits when we should have seen what she was hiding."

"I don't think she'd blame you," Tea whispered.

"No, she wouldn't. But that doesn't excuse it. I failed her, and I failed you." Tears rolled down his cheeks and he swallowed hard.

"I killed her with my selfishness. If I'd been stronger, I could have helped her and helped you, maybe then the accident could have been avoided."

Tea rushed to his side and embraced him. She planted tiny, loving, forgiving kisses all over his face. "Oh, Logan. You can't change what happened. I was drunk and her addiction was out of control." She took a small step backward and stared up at him, her hands gripping his shoulders. "That's why you're so angry. You blamed all of us. Me, your mom, you. Later, when I slipped into full alcoholism, you saw her, echoed in my actions. I think that's why you could never believe I stayed sober."

"I couldn't trust that you'd have the maternal instincts that she lost as the drinking accelerated. My guilt blinded me to the good in you. I've watched you, with Mr. Zed and Destiny and every other person down on their luck. You're there for them, no matter what. I can see it now, the work you put into being generous and being strong for others and you."

He dropped down on one knee.

"Chastity Howell, I'm not going to propose. Yet. However, I'm here, on bended knee, to tell you that I don't blame you for what happened. It was an accident. I'm asking for forgiveness for being an ass, for being blind to my own issues. I've wronged you, you deserve better than me. But I do love you, I never stopped. I'm asking for a chance to start over, to get to know you, to get to know the woman you are today, not the girl I thought you were."

"Yes. Oh yes, Logan," she exclaimed. She drew him to his feet and flung her arms around him. She grasped the back of his head and yanked his mouth to hers. "Yes, Logan Wright, yes to everything." Their mouths met and love and passion exploded around them. Max danced around them yipping excitedly.

Deafening cheers erupted.

Tea glanced around, blushing.

"Oh, I forgot where we were," she laughed.

"Congratulations," Willow exclaimed.

"About time," Mr. Zed called from the back hallway.

"You." Logan pointed a finger at the war hero. "You have an appointment with a psychologist at the hospital. We had a deal. I've lived up to my end; you have to live up to yours."

"Fine," the old man complained. "I'm not going to like it, but I'll do it for Chastity, and for you."

"Can we go upstairs now?" Logan begged. "There's so much to discuss. So much more you need to hear."

"We can." She smiled up at him.

"Mind her virtue, young man," Mr. Zed warned.

Laughing, Logan saluted him and they raced up the stairs, Max barking excitedly at their heels.

Chapter Twenty-Six

Closing the door behind her, Chastity fell into Logan's embrace.

"Max, lie down," Logan commanded gently.

Obediently, Max lay on the floor.

"Stay."

"God, I've missed you," Logan groaned, nuzzling Tea's neck.

"Indeed," she teased, backing away and beckoning at him with one finger. He followed her into the bedroom. She struck a seductive pose on the bed. "Get over here."

He hesitated at the foot of the bed. "Don't take this wrong, but I don't think so. We need to talk."

"Screw that," she laughed. "We've talked enough for now. Actions speak louder than words." She flipped open the top button of her pristine white blouse.

"Tea," he pleaded.

"Logan," she purred his name and flipped open another button.

"Dammit, woman." He scrabbled at his own fastenings and joined her on the bed.

Their lips fused, hands fumbled. One button pinged off the wall and clattered, unnoticed, to the floor.

His kiss was divine. She felt his emotions in the joining of lips, as if he poured his soul into it, telling her without words that she was important to him, that he loved her.

"I love you," she whispered against his chest, sliding lower alongside him, caressing and kissing her way down his body.

"I love you," he echoed, his lips pressed gently on the top of her head. "Get back up here, I wasn't done kissing you."

"It'll wait," she teased, trailing her tongue along the top of his jeans as she tugged the tails of his shirt free.

"Chastity," he warned failing to sound stern.

"Logan," she sighed blissfully. "Shut up. I'm occupied."

"Girl, you're going to drive me to distraction." His hands roamed her curves.

***

"So, my bald hero." She stroked his head.

"I'm not bald." He kissed her shoulder.

"Yet," she teased.

"That's a critical distinction," he informed her.

"Give it up, Logan. You've been losing your hair since you turned nineteen. Male pattern baldness. Fear not, I love it. It's so smooth, sleek, and sexy. Kind of like Jason Statham. Who needs hair when you're as hot as you are?" she asked.

"Not me I guess." He nibbled her collarbone. "We need to get up and talk."

"Mmm," she mumbled as she kissed his ear.

He rolled over, pinning her under him. "We have to talk."

"Fine." She mock pouted.

And talk they did. Late into the night, they talked about their dreams and fears. They shared secrets of their pasts and hopes for the future.

"You need to come to some AA meetings," she said.

"I've been to one."

"When? I didn't see you." She gave him a puzzled look.

"Okay, so I didn't exactly attend. I listened outside the door. I heard you talk about your pain and regret for what happened. Until then, I wasn't sure I believed you…"

"Logan, you can't do that. You can't just eavesdrop. Those meetings are private."

"It wasn't my intention. I went to the public meeting and when I opened the door, I heard you speaking. I listened and I learned. When you were done, I left. I had a lot to think about it."

She huffed. "Well, at least you didn't listen to anyone else. But you need to go to more meetings."

"I plan to. I need to know what I'm up against and how to help."

"What if I fall off the wagon?" she whispered. "I've come close once before. Too close."

"Then I'll drag your ass back up. I know it's not going to be easy. But I know you're worth it. I'm worth it. Worth the risk and the problems. And I know we'll fight," he admitted.

"But not too much," she added optimistically.

"Not too much," he agreed, sealing the promise with a kiss.

"We should get married," she blurted sometime later.

"Let's not rush things," he advised. "Not that I don't want to."

"Rush things? I'm twenty-eight. I've been in love with you since I was ten. The day I met you, I knew I'd marry you. You were such a charmer."

"And you were such a tomboy with the cutest butt."

"Gah, you and my butt."

"You've got lovely curves. Fit and sexy and as hot as hell," he teased, trailing his fingers down her spine. "You don't think it's too soon to set a date?" he asked, returning to her semi-proposal.

"Do you?" she hedged.

"No, I never stopped loving you either."

"So, Saturday then?" she quipped.

"As you wish," he agreed and rolled off the bed.

"Aren't we going to celebrate our engagement?" She smiled up at him, her heart full to bursting.

"Tonight." He leaned in for a kiss. "Technically, I'm at work right now, and if I don't get back soon..."

"Sam will never let you hear the end of it." She laughed.

Chapter Twenty-Seven

"Son, are you sure you aren't rushing this?" Logan's father, Russell Wright, asked, nervously swiping a hand across his completely hairless head. They stood side by side on the front porch of The Tea Shop.

"You can relax, Dad. I wasn't sure at first, and it isn't as rushed as it seems. I've been in love with Chastity since I was twelve." It was difficult to remain patient when all he wanted to do was get married and take off on a two-week honeymoon to Scotland.

"You were right; I needed to get over my anger about the accident. And the self-recriminations."

"I still go to AA meetings to help with my guilt about your mother's death. But I forgave Tea a long time ago. But, what about the drinking?" his dad asked bluntly. "Some alcoholics never recover."

"What I've learned is that there is no recovery. It's a daily struggle to cope. Tea's done phenomenally well; she's been dry, without a single slip for six years. That's an incredible achievement. I've spent hours discussing this with her. There is always a possibility of a relapse, but we're prepared to work together if that happens. It's going to be okay. She's different from Mom. She's stronger. We're going to do this. I hope I have your blessing."

"You're sure then?" His hands fisted and relaxed and he cracked his knuckles. "If you're sure, I'm okay with it."

Logan wrapped his father in a huge hug. They embraced for several moments. "I know it's hard, Dad. I struggled with it for years. I refused to believe it could be true. However, Tea's dry and intends to stay that way. Even when I despised her for the accident and refused to accept that she might have changed, I loved her so much it hurt. She's part of my soul and I can't live without her." He snorted ironically. "For better or worse. We've made it through out first worst—now it's time for our better."

He saw the tension leave his father's shoulders, and knew he'd convinced him that he'd made the right decision.

"All right then. Let's do this. Your brother and sister are inside the shop already."

Chastity straightened the antique lace of her dress. Once white, her grandmother's gown was gently yellowed with age, but fit her to perfection. The silk underskirt rustled when she moved, and the lace arms tickled her wrists. It was her something old. Her something new was the lacy blue and white bustier, panty and garter set she wore under the dress.

"Here," Willow declared handing Tea a sapphire necklace. "Something borrowed, and something blue, besides those sexy panties. No wedding is complete without the entire she-bang. Old, new, borrowed and blue. Now, you're set. I won't ask if you're ready, because I can see that you are. You're giddy with anticipation."

Throwing her arms around Willow, Tea hugged her tight. "Thanks for being with me through all this."

"You know it," Willow laughed. "Although I'm not sure why you wanted to have it here, in The Tea Shop. It's unconventional to say the least."

"We started planning this for the church, but I couldn't get beyond the idea that I was excluding Gran, so Logan said we should tie the knot here." She waved around the storage room that had been temporarily converted to a dressing room.

"Knock, knock," Riley called and opened the door. "All set?"

"Oh gosh yes," Tea exclaimed, "let's do this before Logan changes his mind."

"Girl, there's no way he's changing his mind," Riley laughed. "He's smitten. He's out there pacing. You'd better get a move on."

Tea grinned, ear to ear. "Okay. Ready. Let's go."

Riley, in her sunshine yellow sheath dress, stepped out into the short hallway and waved. The first low strains of the wedding march drifted into the room. Riley winked at Tea and started up the aisle. Willow thrust a gigantic bouquet of pink and yellow roses into Tea's hand and followed Riley.

A last rush of fear chased down Chastity's spine, followed by the certainty that this was right, that this was perfect. Whatever life threw at them, they'd handle it. She'd been through so much, with and without Logan, that she was confident that she could handle virtually anything.

She eased into the hallway and paused before gliding up its short length.

Tea's heart fluttered at the sight of Logan standing by the window. His suit was pristine navy with a light blue shirt and a bright yellow tie that matched the bridesmaid dresses. His smile widened as she stepped forward, each step a bit faster than the last, her haste compelled by the love and passion in his eyes.

She spared Sam, the best man and Brock the groomsman only the briefest glance. Pastor Luke, his leg in a walking cast smiled. Willow and Riley, their faces wreathed in enormous smiles, stood on the other side of the pastor.

Logan stepped forward and grasped Tea's hand, kissing her gently on the cheek.

"No kissing until after the vows, please," Pastor Luke chided gently and the small group gathered for the nuptials chuckled.

Logan mumbled an apology but grinned unrepentantly.

"We are gathered here today..." The words faded into the background as Tea lost herself in Logan's loving gaze.

"Chastity?"

"What? Huh?" she blurted.

"I asked if you take this man to be your lawfully wedded husband," Luke teased.

"Do I ever!" she enthused, "I more than do!"

The pastor looked surprised but behind her, she heard their friends' chuckles.

"Sorry," she laughed. "I got distracted." She smiled into Logan's eyes again. He quirked one eyebrow at her and she realized she was losing her focus again. She tore her gaze away from him and focused on her surroundings. After that, she didn't miss another cue.

It was a good thing that her sponsor, Connie, was recording the wedding, because Tea doubted she'd remember any of it. She was too excited, too ramped up, too much in love to concentrate on anything besides the love glowing in Logan's eyes.

"You may now kiss the bride."

Logan turned her body toward his and cupped her chin in his hand. "I love you, Chastity Howell, or Chastity Wright, you suit me to a Tea, don't ever forget that." He lowered his mouth and captured hers.

The brief, passionate, loving kiss packed a wallop that threatened to knock her on her backside.

"Later on, I'll have you to myself," he whispered in her ear, his breath feathering across her cheek, leaving shivers in its wake. It wasn't his words, or his breath, it was the unbridled passion and love carried in his tone and soft touch. She felt…cherished.

As one, they turned back towards the pastor.

"Ladies and gentlemen, I introduce Mr. and Mrs. Wright. Please join me in congratulating them on this joyous occasion."

Tea slipped her arm into the crook of his elbow as they faced the crowd. "You are my Mr. Right," she whispered as they stepped amongst their cheering friends to accept their congratulations.

And so, their new life together begins.

Other Books by Katie

Contemporary Romance
Rekindled Fire

Contemporary Romance Series
Heart's Haven Series (Resplendence Publishing)
Running Home
Saving Grace
Building Trust (Coming December 2016)

Erotica/Erotic Romance
The Gift
Corralling the Cowboy
Tessa's Trio

The Thurston Hotel Series

http://www.thurstonhotelbooks.com

A Thurston Promise, Book 1
By Brenda Sinclair

Opposite of Frozen, Book 2
By Jan O'Hara

On A Whim, Book 3
By Win Day

Love Under Construction, Book 4
By Sheila Seabrook

A Lasting Harmony, Book 5
By Shelley Kassian

With Open Arms, Book 6
By Moira Stelmack

The Starlight Garden, Book 7
By Maeve Buchanan

Betting On Courage, Book 8
By Alyssa Linn Palmer

The Thurston Heirloom, Book 9
By Suzanne Stengl

An Angel's Secret, Book 10
By Ellen Jorgy

To A Tea, Book 11
By Katie O'Connor

A Thurston Christmas, Book 12
By Brenda Sinclair

About Katie O'Connor

Katie O'Connor lives in Calgary, Alberta, Canada. She married her high school sweetheart and is living her happily ever after. She is the mother of two grown daughters and is extremely proud of her five grandchildren. She has two wonderful sons-in-law and a large support network of friends, family and fellow authors.

Katie's career path has been long and twisted, with most of her life devoted to her family. She's been a waitress, cashier, store manager, as well as a lab and x-ray technician. She is an avid quilter and for a number of years owned and operated a quilting business and designed quilt patterns.

She's dabbled in writing since high school because something drives her to create stories. She swears that it's impossible for her NOT to write. She says, "I think my head would explode if I kept all those ideas trapped inside. My mind is a wildly creative place and all those ideas have to be downloaded to relieve the pressure."

She believes in all things magical including dragons, fairies, UFOs, ghosts, and house pixies. But most of all she believes in love, romance and hope.

Katie likes to make it up as she goes along and dreams of publishing a mixed genre novel. It is going to be an erotic, shape shifter, vampire, steampunk, sci-fi, murder mystery, adventure, romantic, western, historical, thriller with a touch of magic. It will be her biography.

Where to Find Katie

https://www.facebook.com/KatieOConnorWrites
https://twitter.com/katieohwrites
https://www.goodreads.com/KatieOConnor
http://www.amazon.com/author/katieoconnor
http://www.pinterest.com/katieohwrites/
http://katieohwrites.com

As always, Katie loves to hear from her readers.
Feel free to write her at
katieoconnorwrites@gmail.com
She also loves to reward her reviewers. Please send a link
to the above address if you have reviewed one of her
books. She'll enter you in a draw to receive a free book.
And if you'd like to hear occasional news about Katie
and her upcoming books, drop her a line to sign up for
her newsletter.